DEANNA STEWART

Enora Books™

ISBN-13: 978-0-9847174-2-2
Cover art by TONY! Media

To Tony and Tessa:
Your help and encouragement as I completed this book
were invaluable to me.

~ ~ ~

If you, dear reader, are searching for the strength
to break free of a horrible situation, or are celebrating
the freedom you've already fought for and won,
then I dedicate this book to you.

Prologue

During the reign of the great sultans of Persia there were, alas, some sultans who were not so great. Theirs was not the path of justice and prosperity for their subjects, but of power and wealth for themselves alone.

In those times of tyranny, bands of refugees fled their hostile homelands for the safety and freedom of other kingdoms with fair leaders. This was called a *hejira*, and some such journeys became the stuff of legend.

In the region of Bas, which was on the southern border of the great sea, one such legend was told. Bas was most aptly named, for it meant *stop*, and when a traveler arrived at the westernmost part of the region, stopping was all he *could* do, for it became an immense arid desert that no man had yet been able to cross, even with the strongest camel and abundant provisions.

To the north was the huge, bustling city of Enamdar with its towering palace, festive bazaar and many-colored houses, all facing the vast sea which brought merchant ships into port daily. Their cargo was vast and varied – clothing, jewelry, spices, cloth, weaponry, tools, rugs, horses and livestock.

To the east, Etmekstan lay nestled in a verdant valley. Its inhabitants were mostly farmers who loved the land, and whose crops grew in abundance. Its fields were laden with rows of white tufted cotton, lavender saffron crocuses from which the spice of the same name was harvested, and tall rustling stalks of wheat.

To the south, perched on an enormous hill, among dense forests of every imaginable kind of tree, stood the kingdom of Chabouk. Although each realm and its inhabitants had a part to play in the adventure that became legend, it was in Chabouk that our tale began.

Chapter One

Beyond the high walls and massive gates of Chabouk, the marketplace was bustling with activity. Under the mid-morning sun merchants manned their stalls along the dusty winding street and hawked their wares. The air was full of the sounds of the market – sellers calling out to potential customers, hagglers arguing for a lower price, exclamations of delight from women admiring pretty trinkets, and the joyful sounds of children shrieking with laughter as they ran and played.

Along one side of the road were items of adornment and decoration. There were fine Persian rugs of deep blue or rich crimson. They were woven with their signature designs in the center and around the edges – geometric shapes, repeating patterns of diamonds or flowers, or stitching that mimicked the complex and delicate spider web. There was glazed pottery of vivid turquoise or the color of creamy mustard, painted with peacocks strutting in front of trees or great birds standing regally among reeds in peaceful rivers.

Cloth shoes with pointed toes and covered with embroidery or tiny beads sat neatly on a cart. A row of scarves as finely woven and ornamented as the famed Persian rugs rustled prettily with each gentle puff of wind.

Tunics, pants, robes, headdresses and shawls of many colors and a great variety of fabrics were on display. The sun glistened off of the shining jewelry: glass, mother-of-pearl, silver, or gold, fashioned into rings, earrings, circlets, arm bracelets, anklets, or chokers.

Across the path were carts full of delightful smelling food. Fresh, ripe plums were piled next to fragrant, juicy apples and fuzzy peaches. There were tangy onions, bunches of leafy spinach, and roasted pistachios and walnuts. The children favored the dessert stands with crisp, flaky squares of *patisa* and sugar-coated doughy balls of *peda*.

Further up the sprawling hill the tenements were crammed with adobe homes so closely clustered together that a person could reach out of his window with little difficulty and lock hands with his neighbor. They were meager dwellings to be sure, but their owners made them quite cozy by covering the floors with handcrafted rugs, strewing pillows about for lounging, and decorating tables and shelves with pottery they'd made themselves.

At the very peak of the hill sat the royal palace. It was constructed of whitish limestone and had a lotus-patterned brick façade. It boasted nearly a dozen looming towers which were capped, as was the palace dome, with colorful minarets. In it were countless rooms full of lavish furnishings, works of art, fabulous treasures, an expansive garden bursting with flowers, and groves overflowing with trees.

The residence of the royal family was a far cry from the dwellings of the populace. This fact greatly disturbed the kind Panguian Fatima, but not her cruel husband, Sultan Shiraz.

It was in the palace gardens that an anguished wail rang out and shattered the tranquility of the pastoral scene.

"Noooo!"

Fatima had been lounging on the edge of a fountain in the roofless arched courtyard, swirling her hand in the cool water, when she recognized her daughter's cry. Her heart seemed to lodge in her throat, and she leapt up and ran out into the gardens in the direction of the sound. Guards raced behind her, also having heard the cry, but she outpaced them all. She flew past rows of flowers, through a grove of trees and around a little maze of bushes. Oh, why was it taking so long to reach her child?

Finally she spotted the girl kneeling by the pond, sobbing near a lifeless, wet Saluki pup.

It took the woman a moment to catch her breath. Then she bent and gasped. The tawny fur, white flappy ears, and little curled tail told her it was the girl's favorite pet. "Oh no. Beloved, what happened?"

"Th-that awful monster, Prince Mansoor, killed him!" The girl shook uncontrollably and her heart-wrenching cries were so violent that she could barely speak. "H-he had those stupid tassels hanging from his boots and Faarih was only trying to play with them. I hate him!" She leaned into her mother's comforting embrace.

"Shh, my honey drop. It's alright. You saw him do this?"

"Y-yes! I was sitting at my window and I noticed Faarih run up to him a-and try to reach the tassels that were swinging as that oaf walked. He... he only wanted to play. That horrible beast threw my pup in the pond! He was too young to swim! I ran down the stairs and outside, b-but it was so far, no matter how fast I ran! By the time I got here and pulled him out, it was too late! Faarih is dead and that brute killed him!"

Fatima wished she could gather Isla in her arms and carry her inside. She was no longer a babe though, but ten and four summers. So the woman simply sat and rocked her until she quieted.

She helped bury the pup – Isla refused to let the gardeners or guards do it. Only afterwards was she able to draw the girl inside to her room, where she plied her with cups of warm spiced tea and lay in bed with her, stroking her hair until she eventually fell into a fitful sleep.

As they lay among the mass of colorful scattered pillows, they could have been mistaken for sisters, with their olive skin, petite frames and almond-shaped eyes. Only a subtle wrinkle here and there, and a few silver wisps in Fatima's black hair, marked her as the elder. She was thankful, not for the first time, that so little of her husband could be seen in their child.

Painful experience had taught her that being a panguian, a sultan's wife, brought with it none of the happiness, power and influence that most people presumed. It might for other panguians, but most certainly not for her. Shiraz was violent – she had been at the receiving end of that brutality more times than she cared to count. For the most part she had learned to stay out of his way. It was only on behalf of her precious Isla that she still drew the courage to stand before him and plead her case. It was for that reason that she prepared to now.

She climbed quietly from the large poster bed and pushed aside its sheer curtain, smoothed her embroidered tunic, and made sure the single braid that hung to her waist was in place. Then she made her way, with trembling legs, to the chambers of her husband.

Two maids scurried along the long hallway, with its exquisite rugs silencing their steps, and she caught snatches of their whispered conversation as they hurried past a row of huge painted urns.

"What was the commotion I heard in the kitchen yesterday?"

"I helped Amani patch up Prince Mansoor's attendant! The poor man had bruises and cuts and blood everywhere. My stomach still has not settled."

"Oh no! What happened to him?"

"He dropped the prince's trunk when they arrived and clothes spilled onto the ground. Prince Mansoor beat him and kicked him nearly to death, right in front of us!"

"Oh! How could he do something so horrible, and as a guest in someone else's home?"

"I don't know, but his parents acted as if that sort of thing is commonplace. They did not even bother to stop him. They simply looked down their noses at us when they noticed our shock! I say the sooner that cur and his pompous family leave the better. One madman in the castle is enough!"

The women turned a corner and were gone. They hadn't seen their master's wife behind them. She was not angry with them, nor would she have them punished. She knew all too well that they were correct in their assessment of the visiting royal family and of her own unstable husband.

When she arrived at his chambers the sentry on watch bowed.

"Your Majesty, shall I inform the sultan that you request audience with him?"

She simply nodded and waited as the sentinel stepped inside to deliver her message.

When he returned several minutes later and held the door open for her, she was in a mood. She knew Shiraz had purposely made her wait out of careless disregard for her. She took a deep breath. *I must calm myself. This is for Isla.* She composed her features and entered the huge room.

It was an utterly masculine place. The walls were dark, somber colors, there were statues of menacing-looking griffins, gilded tables shaped like elephants, and elaborate tapestries that depicted ancient bloody battles.

She passed by a rather sinister collection of scimitars and approached the divan where her husband lounged. She swallowed. Everything about him was large and intimidating. He was tall and portly with a huge beard and quite bushy eyebrows.

He looked even more menacing in comparison to his thin, elderly vizier, Magus, who was seated nearby. The advisor's frail body looked lost among his voluminous robes and flowing white beard. At the moment he appeared to be reviewing official documents, although she was aware that the old counselor would be listening to every word.

"What is it?" the sultan drawled, as if her presence bored him incredibly.

"I have come to tell you that Prince Mansoor killed Isla's favorite pup in the grove today, and nearly killed his personal servant on the steps of the castle yesterday. I understand that this matter is not as important as issues of state, but his behavior as a visitor in our home is totally inexcusable. None of us would do such a thing if we were visitors in their royal residence at Etmekstan. We may have no right to interfere with the manner in which he treats his people but he at least owes the princess an apology for the death of her pet. She is greatly distraught, and if he does not make amends it will surely not bode well for the purpose of this visit."

"Women!" he spat in disgust. "What makes you think I wish to be bothered with such an inconsequential concern as this? What is a dog to me? Fah!"

Magus leaned forward, and all pretense of perusing his documents was dispensed. "If it pleases Your Highness..."

"Speak," his master commanded roughly.

"Her Majesty has a point – no doubt wisdom gained by being in your enlightened presence. It is a grievous insult for the prince to show such disrespect toward anyone or anything in your dominions in such a manner. Perhaps a discussion with Sultan Burhan about his son's behavior is in order? Surely his father recognizes how he would feel if the slipper were on the other foot. Your illustrious name is known throughout the land, and even the smallest slight, unchallenged, could be seen as a sign of weakness by your enemies."

The ruler rubbed his chin. "Hm, this is true. I will accept your counsel, Magus, and speak with Burhan." Eyeing his mate with a look of irritation he grumbled, "There. You have had your way. Are you satisfied?"

"I do thank you." She took a deep breath. "I truly wish that you would reconsider this arrangement. Mansoor is boorish and without compassion. Why must she marry him when the exalted Caliph has long decreed that women may marry whomever they choose? Besides that, her rightful place is here so that she may someday rule as sultana."

He raised an eyebrow. "I have already made myself clear on this issue. Her rightful place is wherever I put her! As to the *exalted Caliph*," he added scornfully, "He is not here to command me, is he? You failed to deliver my male heir but that does not mean I cannot yet have one." He smirked and chuckled. "As a matter of fact, I may have several already."

"Do you mean to say," she balked with outrage, "That you will ignore the caliph's edict, and exile your own child – and legitimate heiress to the throne – for the sake of an alliance? You would crown one of your sons begotten by a concubine as ruler?"

He narrowed his eyes. "That is precisely what I intend to do. It is my right as sovereign. I have told you before and I tire of repeating myself: I will have no female rule my realm. Now leave me!"

Bowing slightly, she turned and left as swiftly as her legs would carry her. She barely made it to her own bedchamber and slammed the door before she erupted.

"That pompous fool! To think that he will deny his child her birthright to meet his own ends!" She could not be still, and stormed back and forth across the thickly carpeted floor, gesturing wildly. "Then after that arrogant whelp insults her in her home, he will not do as he should for the sake of his flesh and blood, but only so that his *illustrious name* will not be slighted!"

She slumped down at her dressing table and stared despondently in the mirror. She had hoped the prince would be a different kind of man than he'd proven himself to be. That was why she hadn't revealed the nature of his family's visit to Isla yet – in hopes that she might develop affection for him on her own. There was no chance of that now. He was an absolute beast and he had not even grown past ten and eight summers. Violent behavior such as his would likely not mellow with age.

Normally the muted blues and greens of her room reminded her of outdoors and calmed her spirit, but not so now. She was too troubled.

Poor Isla. If Shiraz and Burhan came to an agreement, no amount of objecting on her part would change her husband's mind. She sighed in dread. The girl must be told.

The feast in the great dining hall that night was an extravagant affair. There was a rich stew filled with lamb, fruit and herbs; platters of cheese, nuts and pears; decadent desserts baked with cherries and raspberries, and sweet wine. The women from the harem were brought out to entertain the royal guests. They danced alluringly in their wispy tops and flowing, nearly translucent skirts. The metallic clink of their anklets, belts, and earrings added to the captivating sound of the music.

Isla sat forlornly at the table, oblivious to her surroundings, and barely touched her food. All she could think of was poor Faarih's lifeless body. As soon as was appropriate she retired from the dining hall for the privacy of her chamber. She had nearly reached the stairs when she heard a voice behind her.

"Princess Isla."

She turned, startled, to find Mansoor following her. He leaned his tall, muscular frame against the wall at the foot of the staircase. His dark eyes watched her intently. She stiffened her spine and lifted her chin.

Exasperation covered his face. "Father says I must apologize for the dead dog. I wasn't aware that the thing couldn't swim."

"Then apologize," she replied, glaring at him.

His features twisted in anger, and it was clear that he was not accustomed to being addressed in such a manner. "I just did," he said through clenched teeth.

"No, you didn't," she retorted. "You said you must but you never actually did. Then you had the nerve to excuse your behavior for coming into my home and killing my pet. He was only a babe!" She was mortified to feel tears fill her eyes. She spun around and stomped away. She would not let him see her cry.

He called after her darkly. "Have a care, girl. You can throw as many tantrums as you like here, but it will be another matter when you arrive in Etmekstan. You will do my bidding and I won't tolerate your hysterics."

She spun around in shock and confusion and stared at him as if he had suddenly sprouted a second head from underneath his turban.

His eyes devoured her shapely form and his appraisal was as wholly inappropriate as what he said next. "Father says that all has gone satisfactorily on this visit and I can have you. Then you'll learn to hold your tongue, and you'll be my broodmare. I look forward to it." He turned and sauntered back into the dining hall without another word.

When Fatima went to check on Isla later, she found her shaking and furious. She rushed to her worriedly "Beloved, what has happened?"

Isla folded her arms across her chest. "Why don't you tell *me*? What is happening? Why is the royal family from Etmekstan here? Why is Sultan Burhan in talks with Baba? Why is Mansoor speaking to me so freely and saying that I will be his... his broodmare?"

Fatima went stock still. "He said that?" she gasped with a look of horror.

"Yes. Not long ago, as a matter of fact. So tell me," she said trembling with rage. "What is it that everyone appears to know about but me? I've already guessed. I just want you to actually tell me."

Fatima could not seem to meet her gaze. "Isla, your father and Sultan Burhan have decided that you and Prince Mansoor will wed."

Chapter Two

Three years later

The vizier hobbled along the vast hallway, trying to keep up with his master and the commander of the army, Qasim.

He continued to speak, although he was becoming short of breath from the exertion. "But if you tax the people more, Your Eminence, they will be unable to bear it. We are not like Enamdar, with merchant vessels sailing into port daily loaded with spices and weapons and jewels. The wares our tailors and bakers and cobblers sell will not sustain their families if they are taxed yet again."

The king waved his hand dismissively. "Fah! It is because of cursed Enamdar that the treasury must be strengthened further. I know eventually Karim will try to overthrow Chabouk and make it a province of his wretched city. I have known it for years. That is why this alliance with Etmekstan is so necessary. The marriage of Isla and Mansoor will guarantee an ally when Karim attacks. His armies will not be able to defeat our combined power."

"Sire," Qasim interjected, bowing his elegant frame low in his crisp officer's uniform. "To my

14

knowledge Sultan Karim has in no way ever made any advance upon us."

"You speak the mind of a soldier, but I know the mind of a sultan. He desires my kingdom. By the stars, he shall not have it! Let it be known to all in the village that taxes will be increased immediately! Karim will not best me! Anyone who does not pay all that is due to me will be jailed!"

He stopped and leaned against a wall so that he could rub his foot. "Speaking of cobblers and jail, have the royal cobbler thrown in a cell. These shoes are too tight."

Qasim winced. "Your Highness, he has five children. How will his family survive if he is imprisoned? Would you not rather have him repair the shoes?"

Shiraz stopped massaging his foot, came to stand directly in front of the officer, and spoke barely above a whisper. "The vizier's job is to advise me. Your job is to follow orders exactly as I have given them." Without warning his voice rose to a shriek. *"Now follow them!"*

Qasim's jaw tightened but he spoke not another word. Bowing slightly he turned and stalked down the hallway past the many sculptures of gold, steel and bronze.

Magus shook his head in disappointment at his lord's behavior. At least he could take comfort in the knowledge that the cobbler would not suffer long. Qasim was an honorable man, with more wisdom and sound leadership in one finger than Shiraz had in his whole body. Their master had said to imprison the poor man, but as he sometimes did, he forgot to say for how long. The commander and vizier, in their mercy, always neglected to mention this oversight whenever a citizen was wrongly sentenced by their sovereign. He knew that Qasim would lock the cobbler up for a couple of hours, release him, and then tell him to stay out of sight until Shiraz's wrath died down.

Chabouk's citizens would not fare so well, he thought sadly. The additional tax would be nearly more than their meager earnings could bear, but as with the cobbler, he knew when to speak no more on a matter or risk his king's fury. Instead he changed the subject.

"When is the royal family from Etmekstan to arrive, my Lord?"

"I expect them this evening actually."

"I was not aware it would be so soon. Have the panguian and the princess been informed?"

"No, I have purposely not told them. I have no desire to be besieged by crying females, begging me to reconsider what I have already decreed. They will arrive tonight, we will begin the celebration feast, and three days hence the wedding will occur."

The vizier sighed with an even heavier heart than before. The poor girl! To be kept in the dark about her own future! And her mother's grief would certainly know no bounds after having her daughter snatched from her without warning. Magus' master grew more hot-tempered and suspicious by the day, and his disregard for even his own family was most unbecoming. His volatile moods had become legendary throughout the realm. With a growing sense of dread, he wondered how much worse conditions would grow under the reign of Chabouk's ruler. His thoughts raced but he was wise enough to remain silent. They finally reached the end of the long hallway and began descending the staircase.

Neither he nor his master was aware that Panguian Fatima had rounded a corner behind them earlier in their conversation, or that she now slipped noiselessly inside a nearby room.

Chapter Three

Isla threw a silver hairbrush across the room and watched it graze the wall with a thud and land softly on the carpet. "Is Baba *mad*? Not only does he still mean to force me to marry that awful monster, but he has arranged the wedding for this week without my knowledge?"

Fatima stepped toward her slowly, as if she were a small animal about to bolt. "Beloved, I am sorry. When Mansoor first visited I had hoped that since you must marry, he would at least be someone you could learn to care for if you only got to know him. It was for that reason that I chose not to tell you the cause for his arrival immediately. Then he showed himself to be a brute but it was too late. You had already learned the truth. This time I vowed not to make the same mistake. I told you the moment I learned that he and his family were on their way here in preparation for the wedding." She had to choke out her next words past the knot in her throat. "My heart is full of ache and anger, but your father will have his way in this. You have no choice."

Isla stepped back and tears filled her eyes. "No! I will not do this!"

"It has been three years since you saw Mansoor. It is possible that he has changed greatly during that time," Fatima cooed soothingly with her arms outstretched.

Isla shook her head so vehemently that her ebony braid dangled to her waist like a ribbon in the breeze. "No! Nobody that heartless can change. Baba hasn't." She stomped angrily across the thick Persian carpet, sat at her window and stared despondently at the lush green land below. Rows of rose bushes full of yellow blossoms with spiral centers sent a fragrant breeze wafting up to her room. The tips of red and pink tulips reached up to kiss the sun. She saw none of these things. Her heart was racing like a wild thing and she struggled to gain control of herself once more.

The fear and anguish in her eyes hurt Fatima's heart for she knew all too well that the girl was correct. Still, she felt helpless to change the situation. The marriage was nothing more than a business arrangement between old men bartering their children, as she had heard kings did in other countries, for money or land or alliance in the event of future war. Her husband would turn their precious daughter over to that insolent cur without a second thought.

Fearful determination filled her heart. She never crossed her husband. To do so would bring his wrath, his scathing insults, and his fists down upon her. Still, she had to try. She had long ago accepted her lot and sought comfort in the advantages of being the queen, but she could not allow her daughter to share her joyless and painful fate.

She had to do something to try and get through to him, but what? She stared helplessly at a section of Isla's wall, with its embroidered tapestry. It told an ancient story of inhabitants of three warring tribes who had fled together and established a peaceful empire that no enemy could conquer. Gazing at the design she willed the story of the long-ago adventure in a distant land to give her the inspiration she so desperately sought.

There was a knock at the door, and a maid entered and bowed. "A thousand pardons for interrupting but the royal party from Etmekstan has arrived, and His Highness requires your presence in the dining hall." The two now realized they were being summoned for the beginning of the wedding feast.

Isla rose immediately. They exchanged worried glances as the servant was joined by another and they quickly helped the women change into the garments appropriate for visits of state. Afterwards the mother and daughter clasped hands briefly, and left the room without a word. Their hearts sank as they thought fearfully of the kind of man that awaited them belowstairs, and the kind of future he had in store for Princess Isla.

They entered the dining hall together, both striking in their beauty.

Isla was tiny and slender with chestnut-colored eyes, and full lips that always seemed about to smirk at some mischief. Her tunic was the color of rich mustard and brought out the hue of her olive skin. The silken sash tied at her waist accentuated her feminine shape. Even the plum baggy pants that tapered at the ankle did little to hide the slender curve of her calf. She was adorned as was befitting the special occasion, with a gold crown in her hair, and gold and jewels in her ears, around her neck and on her wrists. Her silk slippers were decorated with intricate beadwork.

Even at her advanced age, the panguian was lovely. She too was slender, but slightly taller than her daughter. Her flowing, waist-length hair was still as black as night, speckled with strands of silver. Her long silver tunic, detailed with embroidery of birds and trees, was tied with a blue sash that accented her tiny waist and matched her blue flowing pants. She too was adorned for the occasion with her crown, jewels and beaded slippers.

They were a fetching pair and everyone in the hall took note, to the delight of the king.

"Such a pretty young lady you've become," the visiting panguian crooned, as if she'd had something to do with it. "You will do quite nicely for my Mansoor." She was shaped very much like an egg and observing her would have been comical if the circumstances had not been so grim.

Mansoor himself simply looked Isla up and down as if she were a tender piece of minced lamb he was longing to wolf down. He was even more imposing than before with his stockier, taller build and strong, angular features. His sour disposition had not changed, and it ruined what could have been a handsome face.

Isla sat on the crimson divan between her mother and future mother-in-law, Panguian Cala, and the sultan signaled for the feast to begin. There was lively music and beautiful dancers and several courses of delicious food – wild pheasant and pilaf, lentils and asparagus, cantaloupe and quince, and an abundance of wine and beer.

The evening would have been enjoyable if not for the fact that it was the beginning of her wedding celebration – a celebration that would end with her marrying the brutish, ogling knave seated between her father and his, Sultan Burhan, who was equally as large and seemed just as moody as his son.

The two women were the picture of grace and they displayed immaculate manners, but Fatima felt her daughter shaking next to her. Every so often she reached under the table and grasped her hand for comfort. It took all her strength to maintain a peaceful and happy façade when she really wished she could burst into tears.

She had always protected her child. She hid the fact that eight-year-old Isla had bullied the groom into teaching her to ride a horse. Shiraz would have been furious. To his mind, a woman was supposed to sit by a window and embroider, not encroach upon the realm of men, even though women in most kingdoms enjoyed great freedom. She saved the child's skin countless times when she would dress up like a boy to climb trees with the servants' children. Once, when she was ten, she was playing near the river and fell in. She would have drowned had Fatima not desperately extended a large branch and pulled her out. That same afternoon they learned to swim together, and none had ever known except her maid, Yusrah, who had been there and had sworn never to tell.

Who would protect her precious baby now? Ten and seven springs had passed since Isla was born. She was certainly more than old enough to marry, and Shiraz had long decided that Mansoor would be her mate. From the preening, haughty demeanor of Panguian Cala, it was clear that her daughter would receive no help from that quarter.

She was pulled from her sad reverie by her husband's outburst.

"Despicable!" he shouted.

"Indeed it is," Sultan Burhan agreed. "They have lain in wait along roadsides, stealing and murdering, and then selling their ill-gotten goods in the next village they ride to. Woe to any who they meet upon the road. They are heartless cutthroats. I deemed it best to warn you that they may be coming here next."

"Does anyone know what they look like?"

"The first has a knife cut across one eye. The other has fashioned his beard into a braid that nearly reaches his waist," Burhan answered.

"I will inform the commander of my forces immediately. If they venture here, they will not leave alive," Shiraz proclaimed loudly.

The news of roaming bandits had put a damper on the evening for those not already miserable. Fatima and Isla were greatly relieved when the dinner was ended, and Panguian Cala declared that she was exhausted from the trip and the wonderful night, and must sleep at once. Fatima had a maid show her to her room and provide whatever she needed. She then hastened to her daughter's bedchamber to speak with her further. When she arrived the door was ajar and she heard the distinct voice of Prince Mansoor!

"Please, you should not be here!" Isla pled.

He smirked and caressed her cheek. "You are beautiful. It's perfectly acceptable for me to be here. We were promised to each other in marriage years ago. Three days hence you will be my bride. You really are already in the eyes of our fathers, so there's no harm in us reaping the benefits of our marriage before the wedding. You've grown even more enchanting since last I saw you." He glanced around the chamber and then started to lead her to the bed. "Come, lie with me among the pillows and let us... talk."

Isla shook her head and stepped away from him, but he grabbed her arm with a cruel grip.

"What is this?" he mused with a frown. "You refuse me? You dare to raise your chin in defiance to me? If your eyes were daggers, I would not live to see our wedding ceremony." His leering gaze turned dark and malicious. "So you have a nasty streak of independence in you. An undesirable trait it will be a pleasure to rid you of."

Isla struggled against him and glanced wildly toward the door.

He only snickered. "Do you suppose anyone will aid you? I already told you: we are practically married. Everyone knows you are mine. They cannot stop me from doing anything I desire to you. You had better get used to it, girl." He gripped her even tighter and she cried out in pain.

Fatima was fuming but she gathered her composure and swept into the room as if she had no idea what was happening. "Isla, beloved, we should talk a final time about what your responsibilities will be now. In all ways you must be pleasing to your hus – oh! Prince Mansoor!" Her face was the picture of innocence and surprise. "Why, what brings you here of all places?"

He released Isla and bowed politely. "Good evening, mother. I was simply allaying Princess Isla's fears about our future together." He turned back to Isla with a cunning smile and deadly eyes. "I look forward to conversing with you more tomorrow. Good night." He bowed and left.

The panguian closed and bolted the door behind him and then ran to Isla, who collapsed in her arms and for the first time in years sobbed like a frightened child.

Through her tears she struggled to speak. "In a m-mansion full of treasures and jewels, what I wished for most was for Baba to love me. I longed for him to h-hug me and kiss me and smile when he saw me enter a room as you do."

Her face twisted in anger and sadness. "What I received instead was indifference unless I was of use to him. I am no more to him than a v-vase or an animal to be traded for greater gain. He will barely talk to me when we are seated near each other in the dining hall. What hope have I that he will hear my pleas and stop this abysmal wedding? None. No hope at all. No hope." Her anguish was too intense for her to continue. She simply cried until her shoulders shook.

Tears fell from Fatima's eyes and pain so great it felt like sickness washed over her. She led Isla to the bed and lay there with her, stroking her hair, singing childhood lullabies, and whispering words of comfort until the princess fell asleep. Then she climbed quietly from the bed and started toward the door. She saw the bolt and stopped. That beast had entered her daughter's chamber before without her consent. If she left the bolt undone, nothing would stop him from doing so again.

She glanced around in thought and spotted the enormous trunk on the floor in the corner. It was nearly ten-foot in length and more than a cubit high, and held her daughter's garments and jewelry. She bit her lip – a lingering sign of her once mischievous spirit. When Fatima stopped worrying, grew suddenly calm, and bit her lip, you could be sure that she was developing a plan.

Silently she crept toward the trunk. It had been at least four years since she had done it. Was Isla truly asleep? The girl mustn't see her. If she knew, there'd be no stopping her from launching a one-woman hejira to escape this abominable situation.

She opened the trunk lid. It was well-oiled and made no sound. Pushing the clothes aside she pulled the tiny, nearly invisible latch that opened the false bottom. After glancing quickly at the bed to be sure Isla was still asleep, she climbed inside and descended noiselessly down the hidden ladder, closing the trunk lid behind her. There was no trace from the inside of the room that she'd ever been there, and no trace from the outside that she'd ever left.

It was dark in the underground corridor but she was not afraid. This darkness had been her ally numerous times, hiding her until Shiraz's fits of rage had subsided.

The secret passages had originally been built to provide an escape route for royal families in case of attack. In the past generation it had been all but forgotten, except by slaves escaping cruel masters and panguians seeking refuge from cruel husbands. The massive ebony wood trunks in each bedchamber were so huge that nobody ever considered moving them, and so the tunnel had never been discovered unless its location was shared in secret, as her mother-in-law, Hadya, had done with a young Fatima.

The former panguian had shown her great kindness and eased the sting of her loveless and lonely existence. Shiraz had followed in the brutal footsteps of his father, Sayed, and the two women had become allies, helping each other endure abusive mates. Hadya had died when Isla was barely able to waddle around, and she still missed her. *At least you are free, my friend*, she thought.

As she traversed the dark channel, here and there she saw faint lights, and knew they were in rooms where someone had a trunk open searching for an item while never realizing what wonders lay just beneath the floor.

She counted carefully and soon reached the ladder she was looking for. She climbed it, lifted the false bottom and pushed past the clothes to cautiously crack the trunk lid. The room was hers and it was empty.

After stepping out onto the floor, she set the trunk in order, changed tunics, and sat at her dressing table. She applied agarwood raisin scent to her wrists and neck, and cooling cucumber salve to her tawny skin.

Just then her maid entered the chamber and jumped in surprise. "Your Majesty! I didn't notice you passing in the hallway."

"All is well, Amani," she said, surprised at how calm she sounded. "Enter."

Seeing her mistress' preparations, Amani rushed over to brush her long black and silver tresses. "Is there anything you wish me to arrange for you?"

The panguian put her blue sash back in place and took a deep, calming breath. "Yes. Send word to my husband that I am on my way to visit him."

She had learned over the years to placate him with soothing words to avoid his wrath, but not so tonight. She stared resolutely into the mirror, and her words were forceful and confident. "There is something I need to discuss with him and it cannot wait."

Chapter Four

Shiraz's mind ran a gamut of emotions. At first he was incredulous that his wife had the audacity to demand an audience with him. Before he could recover from that, she swept into his chambers and caused him to forget the dressing down he'd intended to give her.

Her hair was flowing over her shoulders. She carried with her the scent of sweet, tangy fruit. She had changed clothes and was now wearing a teasing translucent shade of orange, giving him a hint of her lithe form, still sensual after all these years, underneath.

Now he was confused. He was aware that she despised him, yet she sauntered in as if she intended to seduce him. His leering gaze told her that if she chose to, he would most certainly let her.

That was precisely as she had hoped. She might have a chance at gaining his ear if he found her desirable. Nonetheless, the thought of attempting to entice him set her stomach to roiling, and bumps to rise on her arms and neck. Shiraz had not touched her in years, preferring the company of his young, nubile concubines to whet his insatiable appetite. Normally that suited her just fine but tonight she needed his attention and this was the best means to capture it.

She was also relieved to note that the vizier was absent. She harbored no ill will toward him, but he did always seem to be about when one wished to have a private conversation. She approached the divan he was lounging his corpulent self upon, still in his robe and turban from dinner, and sat upon a settee on the side near his head. She did not care to be near his pudgy feet, which were dangling from the edge of the couch. She remembered vividly the sting of those pointy-toed sandals from the times when he had kicked her.

"What is this thing that cannot wait?" he asked gruffly.

"It is about Isla. I hoped we might talk a little about the wedding and how you think she and her betrothed will get along."

The king rolled his eyes and all of his desire was immediately quenched. "Not this again. What do I care whether they get along or not? Burhan and I have already agreed that the marriage will happen. That is all that matters."

"I understand," she answered quietly. "But, she is your only child. Surely you have wondered how she feels about the man she will soon marry."

"Fah!" he scoffed, waving his hand in disdain and popping a grape in his mouth from a bowl on a silver pedestal. "Women's emotions change by the moment. What has that to do with anything? I see your game. You approach me trying to look desirable so that you can bend my ear with girlish nonsense about love and –"

"Why is love nonsense? My parents were madly in love." Her voice quavered. "I once tried to love you."

"Your parents fawned all over each other like young, insensible lovers. You foolishly tried to drag me into such ridiculous displays and I wisely refused."

She rose suddenly. "Why should they not have been lovers? They were married! They cared deeply for each other, they loved me and they believed they were sending me to a home where I would have what they had. It is a shame that they were so sadly mistaken."

"They were weak and foolish. You were well rid of them."

"No! What they had was strong and enduring. If they had known the kind of man you truly were, they would never have allowed the marriage."

Shiraz glared at her menacingly. "And what kind of man is it that I truly am?" he asked, slowly beginning to rise from the divan.

The panguian struggled to reign in her emotions. She had intended to win him with honeyed words, not lose her temper. His careless slander of her beloved parents had been more than she could bear. *I need to control myself. I am here for Isla.*

She knelt by the divan and looked up at him. "Please, I meant no harm. Isla is frightened of Mansoor. She knew him to be cruel in his youth and she fears he has not changed for the better since then."

He nodded in approval as he wiped the sticky grape juice from his hands onto his robe. "Firmness and strength are necessary to rule a kingdom."

"Strength, yes, but cruelty, no!" she cried. "There is a great difference. Also, he has taken no interest in getting to know her. He hardly even speaks to her – only stares at her as if he cannot wait to devour her."

"They will have plenty of time to learn about each other after they are married, and it is common for a man to desire his future wife," Shiraz argued.

"She is not his wife yet, but he wishes to take liberties with her as if she already is! I discovered him in her room today attempting to lay with her! She was terrified! That was utterly inappropriate!"

"I don't see how. They have been betrothed for years, and the wedding is in three days. In the eyes of many, they are already married. Be gone with you and all of this foolishness."

Fatima rose with fury in her eyes. "So you would have him strip her of her virtue against her will? You are her father! You are supposed to protect her!"

Shiraz jumped up and waved his arms wildly. "I *am* her father and it is my duty to arrange for her marriage in a manner that benefits both cities!"

"Even if it means your only child will suffer?" She was crying and shaking now.

His shrug reeked of indifference. "She is a woman. It is her lot to suffer. You of all people should know that," he added tauntingly. "Now I have already told you: leave me, and take your petty concerns with you!" He sat down and ate another grape, already having dismissed her in his mind.

Years of pain at his hateful words and stinging blows, countless tears and loveless days, all welled up inside so suddenly that her emotions burst forth and she realized to her horror that she could not contain them.

"Oh yes, I know. You played the charming prince with my parents and gained their trust, only to reveal your true nature after you had me trapped in this castle. You treated me worse than a dog, taking my affection and dashing it to the ground."

"I commanded you to leave!" he snapped, but she could not stop.

"Whenever I showed an ounce of strength, intelligence, or independence, you hurled your insults and fists at me, until I learned to fear you. I cowered in your presence and wished for death. I hoped Isla's birth would soften your heart, but you have no heart! You viewed her as an irritating responsibility. She offered you her unconditional love and you cast it aside as callously as you rejected mine. You never deserved our devotion!"

He rose from the divan again and waddled down the stairs toward her. "You will hold your stupid tongue!"

"You care nothing for your family, your army, or your subjects," she blazed on. "Not the poor who struggle in the streets, or the soldiers you prepare for senseless wars, or the hard-working servants you've had tortured for making the simplest of mistakes. Your power has gone to your head and addled your senses. Shiraz cares only for Shiraz. You believe you are untouchable, but *nobody* is untouchable – not even you. One day you will find yourself in a situation where your influence, your army, and your riches will not be able to save you. Your only rescue will have to spring from those who love and respect you. Woe to you then, mighty sovereign, for people fear your cruelty, envy your power, and tolerate your presence, but *nobody* loves and respects you."

Every inch of him screamed with fury as he reached for her. "It has been a great while since I have had to show you your place. It appears you have grown overconfident and I will have to remind you!" He brought his beefy hand around and struck her with such force that she fell backward onto the floor.

She raised her arms to block the blows as he attacked her again and again, striking her anywhere he could, except for her face. It wouldn't do for her to present herself before their guests with bruises which could be seen.

The sentry outside the door heard the tussle and called out. "Your Majesty, do you require my assistance?"

He leaned against the tapestried wall heaving from the exertion. "Escort my wife to her chambers," he called out in a tone dripping with contempt.

He sneered at her, as if he enjoyed the sight of the bruises deepening on her arms. He cackled oddly and something unstable flashed in his eyes. "Another foolish outburst like this and you'll receive far worse and you'll be confined to your chambers until after the wedding. That way there'll be no chance for the both of you to conspire any further."

"No! Please don't!" she pleaded through her tears, but he turned his back to her and returned to his divan and lay down.

The sentinel entered and swiftly surveyed the scene, but said nothing. He lifted his queen from the floor and escorted her out. After they reached the hallway and he had closed the door, his tone and demeanor softened. "Can you walk, Your Majesty?"

Nodding wordlessly she leaned on him for strength as he escorted her to her room.

His expression was troubled. "Would you like for me to send your maid to... assist you?"

She shook her head. "No, I will tend to myself. Thank you for your kindness. I wish to be alone."

He bowed and stepped aside for her to enter, and then closed the door behind her.

Once inside, she stood bracing herself against the wall and breathing deeply until the shaking and dizziness stopped. For long moments she gave in to hot, angry, fearful tears.

In quiet desperation her eyes darted around for a sign, some idea of what to do. The image on the tapestry in Isla's chamber sprang into her mind. What was the story? She willed herself to remember, and bit by bit the tale became clear again in her mind. Her gaze rested on the trunk. She stood up straight and bit her lip.

Chapter Five

Budmash was a desolate place.

It wasn't even supposed to be there. It was part of no neighboring kingdom and none claimed it. It was not sufficiently close to Etmekstan to the east for it to be of any concern to Sultan Burhan. To the west was only desert. Sultan Karim of Enamdar to the north greatly desired to make it a safe oasis for weary travelers, but it was a bit too far beyond his boundaries for him to make it his province. Chabouk to the south was nearest to it but Sultan Shiraz cared for nothing that did not increase his fame. If Budmash did not bother him, he did not bother it.

So there it sat slightly off the middle of nowhere. It consisted of little more than a sprinkling of ramshackle stucco buildings and small groupings of market stalls. Its inhabitants were disreputable vendors; purveyors of hard liquor and willing women; dirty, barefoot children – most of them orphans, and mangy, half-starved dogs. There was an inn with only a couple of rooms that sold weak wine and bland food; a tavern that doubled as a brothel; and a jail run by a self-appointed kuipan who probably should have been behind its bars.

He should not rightfully have even been called a kuipan for that title was supposed to belong to the superintendent of a city's police force. Budmash had no police force. Thieves and miscreants found a haven of sorts there. Most honest travelers tried their best to avoid it altogether, and instead went further north, south, or east to more hospitable lands.

The two fellows on the road just outside of Budmash were no honest travelers, and the last one they'd encountered now lay dead at their feet.

Omar was nearly a giant. He stood two heads taller than most men, was massively broad of build, and had an ugly slice mark across his right eye. His black vest, pants and sharp-pointed boots matched his dark disposition. Mustafa was smaller in stature, but deceptively nimble and no less treacherous than his partner. His braided beard swung like a rope down his chest, all the way to the waist of his crimson tunic.

Omar peered into the poor man's bag to survey their spoils. He rubbed his bald head in disgust and let loose a filthy string of expletives. To his friend's raised questioning eyebrow he responded in his impossibly deep voice, "All this fool peddler had was a few piddling coins, some worthless dishes, and pots! Killing his worthless hide wasn't even worth the trouble!" He spat in disgust and wiped his bloody blade on the dead man's pants.

Mustafa shrugged. "Such is the lot of a bandit. Sometimes it's jewels and gold; others it's spoiling fruit and ragged clothes." He pulled the shoes from their victim's feet and tucked them in his own bag. "We wouldn't have stayed in this business if the good hauls weren't worth the occasional bad ones, ay?"

The giant chuckled as he searched the merchant a final time for anything valuable. "Ay, this is true. You missed your calling. You should have been a philosopher instead of a thief."

After unceremoniously divesting the poor man's body of its belongings, they simply left his corpse there to be dealt with by the animals and the elements. They now sought to turn a profit for their grim wares among the rickety market stalls of the place whose inhabitants called no man their sultan.

This had been their pattern for months now as they cut a bloody swath across the country, from further east than even Etmekstan. The bandits tethered their horses and walked toward the market. They were an intimidating pair, even in a place such as Budmash, and all who passed them in the street gave them a wide berth.

They strode along the stalls for nearly an hour, selling a scarf here and a jug there until they had sold most of the goods from their latest robbery. It was then that something caught Omar's eye. His glance darted around the street for several seconds before he spoke again. "Say, have you noticed the little street urchins running about since we arrived?"

Mustafa glanced around and noted several skinny boys of all ages and sizes throughout the marketplace. "Now that you mention it, there are a lot of them, aren't there?"

"Yes, and most of them are very talented at stealing food and picking pockets," Omar observed in amusement.

They lounged near the corner of a hovel and watched the children. Some ran through the streets, chasing each other in play and laughing.

Eventually the chasee would bump into a fellow, and offer "a thousand pardons" as the chaser relieved the unwitting victim of his moneybag.

Near the fruit stand, a child argued with the vendor about the price of a cantaloupe. While the owner was shooing him away, another waif slid several pears into his tunic and slipped into the crowd unnoticed.

Omar roared with laughter. "I do believe what we are witnessing is a band of organized robber boys!"

Mustafa snickered. "Indeed. Hold tight to the moneybag, big one. These bandits are not to be trifled with."

Every so often a child would be caught in the act and get his ears boxed, and the pair guffawed at that too.

Eventually it started to get dark and they grew tired of their entertainment, so they went in search of a tavern with good, strong drink and harlots. They sat and drank until late into the evening, talking and listening to the tales travelers brought in.

"What news from Enamdar?" one merchant asked another as they scraped chairs away from a table and sat.

"The bazaar is full of treasures, as always," the man answered. "Oh, and a merchant vessel sank near the harbor last eve. Few on board survived and most of their wares are now at the bottom of the sea. Sultan Karim is offering aid to the survivors in returning to their homelands. What comes of the south?"

"The wedding of Princess Isla of Chabouk to Prince Mansoor of Etmekstan takes place three days hence. The city is abuzz, although not all are excited. It seems the prince is quite wicked. The citizens adore their princess and so despise her future husband."

"Understandably so," replied the merchant who journeyed from Enamdar. "I've seen my share of wicked princes who become wicked sultans. That is why I like Sultan Karim. He is honest and fair, and has taught his sons to be so. When he is gone, the people will continue to prosper."

His friend nodded in approval. "That is as it should be. I'll be glad when I get there. This is an evil place."

Omar finished eavesdropping, drained his last cup and wiped his mouth with his sleeve. "To the west is only barren desert. It is either north or south, my friend, before leave Bas and returning east. Which shall it be?"

Mustafa stroked his long beard thoughtfully, mulling over what he'd heard. "The sunken ship promises great treasure for those willing to swim and search for it, but I'll wager scores of people are already wading through those waters at this moment. Too much competition for my taste. However, a kingdom preparing for a royal wedding will be far more... distracted. A couple of foreign merchants ought to be able to get in quietly, make quite a bit of gold and slip out unnoticed during the celebration."

Omar swatted him hard on the shoulder. "I like your way of thinking! Not only a philosopher but a strategist as well! So be it. Tomorrow we ride for Chabouk!"

As he stroked the hilt of his scimitar he lowered his voice and a sinister grin spread across his face. "And it's a sorry morning for whoever we meet along the way."

Chapter Six

Raheem and Mahmood strolled along the garden path together deep in conversation. The princes were on their way to the council meeting with their father, the vizier, and the captain of the guard.

Sultan Karim was sitting at his window gazing at the sea, as was his habit, when he noticed them and smiled, his gentle eyes wrinkling at the corners. They were tall and broad like him, with hair the color of the blackest night as his had once been before his increasing age turned it silver. Several maidens eyed his sons discreetly as they passed. The king observed this and chuckled. They would have no problems finding wives.

He always enjoyed the quiet moments he could spend seated on the padded bench at the sill. The warm sun soothed his aching muscles and the gently rolling waves eased his spirit. His empire was vast and he was seldom able to unwind, but when he could steal away, this was where he went to find peace.

His smile faded and he sighed, overcome by a wave of melancholy. "Ah, Lida, my sweet wife, I miss you terribly since your passing. You would be so proud of our sons. I know I am. Raheem will

41

be a wise ruler when I am gone. Of this I have no doubt. Mahmood too is strong of character, and I trust his judgment as much as that of his brother. I am twice blessed. If only you were here to share it with me, there would be none happier than I."

He rose and stretched his tired body. He could not linger in seclusion. It was time for the meeting. He took a last look out of the window, smiled at the sight of the princes laughing about some jest or other as they entered the great hall, and then he left his chamber to join them.

"Father," Raheem began. "It was noble and honorable of you to seek out the survivors of the merchant vessel that took on water and sank. It saddens me to think how close they were to safety: within sight of our shore."

"Yes, sire," agreed the vizier, Ihsan. "It is a very grievous thing that so many lives were lost. Nonetheless, your aid to the survivors has been most bountiful."

Karim sighed. "What else could I do in good conscience? Most lost all the treasures they had traveled to sell, and so were without money or the wares of their livelihood. I was glad to offer Enamdar's assistance. Providing food, lodging, care for their wounds and return passage to their homeland was the right thing to do."

He turned to Mahmood. "What of the treasurer? For those survivors who were able to salvage a portion of their goods, has he been making sure to pay a fair price for them?"

Mahmood nodded his head. "Yes, Father. Thanks to your edict, they will return home with something besides their lives."

"Your Majesty," the deep-voiced Captain Hasan addressed Sultan Karim. "I dislike bearing ill tidings, but there is still much to be done. My sentries have reported that scavengers have been swimming out to grab whatever treasure they can find."

Karim's face darkened. "That is inexcusable! Those poor travelers have already lost nearly everything. If any valuables are recovered, they must be returned to their rightful owners."

Hasan nodded. "I have doubled the guard along the shore, both day and night. We will put an end to their thieving."

"Excellent, Captain. Are there any further items to discuss?"

They talked of trade, troublesome Budmash, which was the bane of every decent traveling merchant, and irrigation improvements for the city. At last the meeting ended, and the captain and vizier parted to return to their respective duties.

Karim walked in companionable silence with his sons, each of them deep in thought. He realized that every city had disreputable characters, but through diligence and just laws he was able to make Enamdar safe for his subjects. Of this he was proud, but as his pained joints protested with each step over the cobbled stone, he also recognized that his body was wearing down.

He glanced affectionately at the princes. He had begun looking forward to the day when he could pass the reins of leadership to Raheem, and then spend warm afternoons sitting in the garden and watching the sea. He could imagine himself napping in the sun or bouncing a future grandchild on his knee.

He chuckled aloud and the men looked at him questioningly.

He smiled at them. "Ah, what a sentimental old fool I've become." They saw the tenderness and pride in his eyes, understood, and returned his fond gaze.

"Well, at my age, with all I have seen and been through, I am allowed to be."

The three men laughed as they parted ways, and Sultan Karim returned to his peaceful window seat overlooking the sea.

Chapter Seven

"Isla, beloved, wake up."

The sound pulled Isla gently from her slumber, and she groggily opened her eyes. "I-I'm sorry. I didn't mean to fall asleep."

Fatima touched her cheek. "You have had an exceedingly trying day. I do not begrudge you a moment of your peaceful rest. Come, arise so we can talk."

The urgency of her mother's tone shook off the vestiges of her fatigue. She sat up and then gasped. "Your arms, your neck! Wh-what happened?" Tears burst forth and she covered her mouth to trap her cries of dismay.

"I talked to your father on your behalf as you slept. I begged him not to force this contemptible marriage. He refused and mocked your fears. He... said hateful things. I have endured his cruelty for years and kept silent. I accepted my fate, but I refuse to allow him to destroy your future too!"

Her anger arose anew and she stood and began to pace the floor. "I could not contain my rage, and I spoke from my heart. He did as he has always done when I dared speak truth to him: he silenced me with his fists."

"Oh please forgive me!" Isla cried. "In my heart I was angry with you. I believed that you would not try to help me, that you were a coward. Now here you stand, bruised and battered because of your courage and love for me. I am so sorry!"

Fatima rushed to her side. "Shhh, my honey drop," she whispered, gathering her into her arms, despite the pain the bruises caused. "This has happened many times before. I hid much from you through the years, to protect your young mind. I have always protected you." Quiet determination filled her voice. "I will protect you now."

She clasped Isla's face in her hands. "What I have to say breaks my heart, but there is no other way. Earlier today I pondered whether you might attempt to run away to escape this marriage. Now I realize that is exactly what you need to do. You must leave while it is night."

Isla tried to protest but she would not be swayed. "Start afresh in another country. Things are not restricted for women in other places as they are for us here. There are many honorable ways for you to make your way in the world. You will not have the luxuries of a princess, but you will be free to choose your own path. You must obey me in this."

Both women were crying now and Isla squeezed her hands. "But if I do this, I – I could never return! I would not see you again, for Baba would realize my treachery and –"

"I know – he might kill us both. But if you leave with Mansoor, I will still likely never see you again, for if he cannot break you he will kill you. At least this way, I can take comfort in my loneliness knowing that you are safe. If I believed there were any other means I would tell you, but there is not, treasure of my heart."

Isla's face was wrought with torment, but suddenly it held a glimmer of hope. "Leave with me," she pled. "Baba will suspect you when he finds me gone. You will surely suffer his wrath."

Fatima shook her head sadly. "No, I cannot. You will move more briskly without me slowing you down, and I can help you better here. I can keep your absence a secret long enough for you to get far away, and I can throw them off of your trail once they do discover that you are gone. I am accustomed to Shiraz's wrath. I have survived this long. I will continue to do so. I want more for you than survival. I want you to *live*. There is a very great difference. You must leave tonight, and you must leave alone."

The matter was settled. They embraced and wept bitter, sorrowful tears, whispering words of affection in the dark room.

Finally Fatima rose. "Come, we have to prepare. You will leave within the hour." She reached for a satchel Isla hadn't noticed sitting on the floor, and placed it on the bed.

"I remember this!" Isla pulled out an outfit meant for a boy – it had belonged to a male servant and she had lifted it years before on washing day. "I used to dress up in this and go on all sorts of adventures!"

"I remember too," Fatima replied, tongue-in-cheek.

"It just disappeared. I searched everywhere for it. I always wondered what happened to it."

"*I* happened to it. You were in too many scrapes for my comfort and I was terrified that your father would catch you eventually so I hid it. I had no idea why I didn't just burn it, but now I know. You will take this with you. It is not safe for a lady to be unescorted. This will suffice as a disguise. You have filled out, but I believe it will still fit. There is money in here, food from this evening's dinner, and a jug of fresh water."

She pulled several scarves and pieces of gold jewelry laden with diamonds and emeralds from a bag inside the satchel. "These are the things you will sell at bazaars along the way to provide for your journey. They are common enough items that nobody would recognize as mine. We cannot get you a horse without being seen so you will need to make the first part of your journey on foot. Since Budmash is closest, start there. It is just on the other side of the forest, and you can reach it within two hours if you do not slacken your step.

When you are near the city put on your disguise and buy a horse or camel from the market. There are more than enough valuables in this bag to purchase one so that you may hasten your journey. Then ride swiftly to the port city of Enamdar. The ruler there is kind and virtuous, and merchant ships come and go daily from distant lands. I have heard that they even sail to places beyond the vast desert and trade with domains there. Nobody would consider searching for you beyond the western wasteland, and certainly you would not be discovered if you flee across the sea. Find a boat that will carry you far from here, purchase your passage and fly!"

Isla ran to her trunk, pulled out bracelets, rings, and other trinkets she didn't wear, and added them to the bag. Neither of them could think of another thing to add, and Isla wasn't sure she could even carry the satchel if it grew too heavy.

"How will I get out? Through the window?" She went to the opening and peered doubtfully at the ground below.

"Certainly not! You will not climb down from some high wall, only to fall and meet your end before you ever leave the castle grounds." She returned to the trunk the princess had just left, pushed the clothing aside and lifted the false bottom. "That," she said to an open-mouthed Isla. "Is what secret passages are for."

Despite the dire situation Isla could not help but laugh in surprise as she peered into the darkness beneath the trunk. "Why didn't you ever tell me about this?"

Fatima laughed as well. "You cannot be serious! I just told you that I hid things from you for your protection. This is exactly such a thing, but not only for your safety. With all the trouble you were forever getting into, showing you a secret passageway would have been disastrous, and it would certainly have no longer been a secret. When I came here, Hadya, your grandmother, was the only person who showed me kindness. It was she who told me about the passageway. It was a refuge when she needed to hide from her own husband, and where later, I would learn to hide from mine. I could not risk you revealing the secret in childish carelessness."

Isla nodded solemnly. "I understand. I am sorry that I caused you such trouble all these years."

Fatima hugged her. "You never did know your place. If you were aware of it, you refused to stay in it. You got that from me. I learned painfully to stay in my place eventually." She kissed Isla's forehead. "May you *create* your place in the world and choose your own destiny."

They climbed partway down the ladder, with Fatima moving gingerly, for she was sore from her husband's thrashing. They ensured that the trunk lid was firmly closed, and began their journey through the passageway. Taking her daughter's hand, she latched it onto her tunic, wordlessly indicating that she had to hold onto it so that they could stay together in the dark.

Isla nodded and they moved forward. Soon they could see faint lights here and there, and hear conversations in rooms they passed overhead. Then Isla realized why her mother was so quiet – their movements might likewise be heard as easily! She remained silent despite the myriad questions that flew through her mind.

The minutes seemed to turn into hours. Yet with the sure foot of one who had traveled this path before, Fatima passed several ladders under the dim light from above until she approached one that, to Isla, looked the same as all the others. She stopped, held her finger to her lips to ensure Isla's continued silence, and moved up the ladder.

It was too dark to see where they were, but Fatima crawled out of the secret opening and Isla followed. She felt prickly sensations brush along her neck and shoulders, and moments later, she was being helped to her feet.

Isla gasped. They were outside, at the edge of a grove of evergreens beside a high wall. The secret entrance was covered by brush, and she realized that the poking she'd felt was from the branches of a bush. They were completely outside of the gates of the city! She was coming to understand her home, and her mother, in a whole new light – just as she was forced to leave them both. Tears sprang to her eyes as they embraced. "I love you, Maman!" she said softly.

"I will always love you, my precious Isla," Fatima answered through her own tears.

They embraced and gazed tenderly into one another's faces. Finally mother stepped away from daughter. "Go. Be free."

With a last longing look Isla turned and crept into the woods.

It seemed to Fatima that on the other side of the wall the entire kingdom was asleep. From the castle with its ornate archways and turrets, to the village further down the hill with its homes, shops and inns, she heard only quiet.

Nearly blinded by her pain, she noticed none of the eerie beauty of her surroundings. Instead she stumbled to the hidden entrance behind the bushes, and crawled back into the secret passageway. She wanted to lie there on the cool floor and succumb to her tears, but she could not because she would be detected from above. Besides, she told herself, there would opportunities aplenty for crying later, but for now, she had to find Shiraz and make sure there was no suspicion that Isla was gone.

She muffled a sob, took a deep, resolute breath, and began the lonely journey back. Shakily, she crept through the tunnel and counted ladder after ladder until she reached the secret entrance to the room she was looking for. Her heart slammed wildly in her chest.

At all costs, she must not be caught! She held her breath in hopes that the hinges would not squeak, stepped gingerly up the rungs until she reached the top of the ladder, and pushed.

Chapter Eight

The false bottom lifted up noiselessly. A few turban cloths and tunics slid silently aside and Fatima raised her head into the trunk, careful not to climb up too far, and lifted the lid. She balanced herself, stood motionless on a ladder rung and listened. The first thing she heard was a female's petulant voice.

"But when, my love? How long must I wait in the shadows, sneaking moments of passion with you?"

There was a rustling of bed sheets and then Shiraz chuckled. "Not much longer now. Isla will be married at the week's end. Perhaps a month later I will announce that my wife, with her weak constitution, has gone mad with grief because of the departure of our precious child. I will have her confined to the farthest tower and closely guarded, for her own safety of course."

"Your subjects will feel poorly about you if we make our devotion known while they believe the queen is ill, my lord."

"That may be so, but those who are mad often harm themselves or end their lives. If, by some such unfortunate event, she should meet her untimely end – and I rather think she shall – I will be a mourning, lonely monarch, yes my dove?"

The courtesan practically purred. "Mmm, and then I will come forward to comfort you, be your new queen, and give you a son who will reign someday?"

"Yes, yes. Continue to please me and it will be just so."

"Oh, I shall," came the seductive response. "I will continue to please you even now, my lord."

Shiraz laughed again and then moaned, and Fatima stayed to listen no more.

Stepping down into the corridor she held onto the wall for strength. Was it not enough that he had beaten her until her body was nearly covered in bruises? Now the blackheart would feign her insanity and murder her, replacing her with his mistress? So great was her shock and rage that she could hardly keep from trembling!

Her mind was racing now. *What a fool I've been, believing I would be safe, when I might have flown with Isla and been free from this animal!* She returned to her chamber and leaned against the wall, willing her nerves to calm and allow her to think.

Only a few seconds had passed when she suddenly bit her lip and a look of determination washed over her face. *It may already be too late but I must try to fly still! I cannot waste another moment. I may yet catch her! Not a one-woman hejira after all!*

She had no disguise as Isla had, and she had already given her what jewelry could be sold without suspicion. After all of today's treachery she had no appetite and there was no time to sneak to the kitchen again anyway, so she packed no food. She simply rolled a cloth into a sort of satchel with a change of clothes and shoes inside, gave a final look at the room that had been more a prison than the chambers of a queen, and again snuck out through the secret passage. This time after the long walk through the channel, it was she who slipped into the forest toward Budmash. She did not look back.

Her heart was filled with fear, excitement and hope, but also with a tinge of sadness. The subjects of Chabouk – mothers with their giggling barefoot children playing in the streets, wizened men chatting near the city gates, merchants hawking melons and limes and dates – they had been her people. As a panguian she had only been the wife of the sultan, not a sultana herself with power to rule, but she had cared for the welfare of those under Shiraz's reign.

"Be well," was the blessing she whispered as she strode among the giant oaks. Through the canopy of their massive branches she glimpsed the black night sky with stars scattered across it like jewels.

She noticed a tree with a sort of split trunk, causing it to look like a giant ragged slingshot. In her mind she saw Isla hanging upside down from such a tree in Chabouk as a child, and she smiled. *Oh, please let me meet her soon!*

Step by step, passing tree after tree and bush after bush, she kept moving forward. Her muscles and joints ached from her encounter with Shiraz, and as the journey lengthened, more than once she wondered if she could finish what she had started. Finally she arrived at a bend in the forest and spotted a river. Her heart was greatly lightened, for from this she realized that at last she was more than halfway to Budmash! She started to whisper her daughter's name, hoping she was nearby, when she heard the whinny of horses. Someone was coming!

She glanced around desperately and noticed a tree with a huge gnarled root that had grown up out of the ground, arched and sunk back into the earth. *Aching joints, do not fail me!* She stepped onto the root and grabbed a wide branch above her head. After slinging her pack onto the branch she swung her battered limbs, with no great grace and a large amount of clumsiness, into the leaves. Some of them fluttered to the ground, snapped loose by her passage, and then it looked as if nobody had ever passed the tree.

Concentrating on steadying her breath so that she made no sound, she sat motionless. Just in time! Voices rang out in the night air, grew nearer, and moments later from her hiding place she saw a pair of men ride up and dismount. As they watered their horses she got a look at them. They were both dressed as merchants, but not prosperous ones. Their clothes were dirty and frayed and their turbans carelessly wound.

One was tall and stocky and the darkness hid his features from view. He told a bawdy joke, and the other man guffawed. From the angle he stood at, the moonlight made the second fellow easier to see. He was not as large as his friend and his black beard swung in a braid down his chest. The bandits Sultan Burhan had spoken of!

At the moment she was about to let out a gasp of shock a hand came forward from the darkness and covered her mouth.

There was a desperate whisper in her ear. "Sh! Do not struggle or bite me! If you do, we will both fall and all is lost! It is I, Isla!"

Fatima could have wept with relief but danger waited outside their door. She nodded without turning around, to show she had understood, and then the hand left her mouth. They silently watched the travelers standing by the river. Until that threat had passed, there could be no further reunion.

"See how this water's current flows back towards Budmash? That means its source is in or near Chabouk, so there will likely be lush forests in that direction. I say we go a little further upstream and bed down for the night out of sight behind a cluster of rocks or among the trees," the tall one said. "We may wake in the morning to find our next appointment coming down the road."

Braided Beard cackled. "Ay, Omar. We can lighten his load, have a bit of fun with him, and then it's off to market at Chabouk." He rubbed his hands together, obviously enjoying the thought of the next morning's robbery. "I hope whatever the poor fool is carrying is worth more than the last fellow. I crave good old gold mina! Those meager shekels were barely sufficient to purchase that unimpressive dinner and those watered down spirits at the tavern. Not even enough for a night at a half decent inn, wenches or passable wine!" He looked affronted, which set Omar to laughing as they meandered further up the river to make their beds for the night.

The women waited for several minutes afterwards before either uttered a word, and even then, they spoke in whispers.

Fatima turned carefully so as not to lose her seating and faced her daughter.

"I am so glad you are here," said Isla. "Truly we have been protected this night! I had almost reached the end of the forest and was near the road to Budmash when I heard riders coming at a leisurely pace. I could not tell who they were but their conversation troubled me so I doubled back and climbed this tree to hide until they passed. When we saw them I realized that they are the very thieves we learned of."

Fatima hugged her tightly, overcome with joy that the cruel outlaws had not overtaken her daughter.

They sat facing each other. "Maman, I will be forever grateful that you are here, but what changed your mind?"

With sorrow and anger the older woman repeated the conversation she'd overheard in her husband's bedchamber, and when she was done Isla was so furious that she could not speak for a moment. When she finally regained her composure, she replied resolutely.

"Look overhead. Night has passed into early morning. The nightmares of our past are over. With the dawn of this day we both leave our monsters behind."

"You have spoken wisely, my child. We should wait a little longer to be sure the thieves are asleep, and then hurry to Budmash." She sighed and shook her head. "I do not like imagining what will happen to the person who passes this way after us. He will not reach the city gates."

Isla grew silent and twirled the end of her long braid with her fingers.

"What are you plotting?" her mother asked suspiciously. "You look as if you are hatching a wild scheme."

"I *am* hatching a wild scheme! What if... what if we did something that is dangerous to the point of madness, but which – if we survived – could both keep anyone from trying to find us ever again, and stop those despicable villains from robbing and killing anyone else?"

Fatima folded her arms. "You will have to understand that all I have just heard is 'dangerous to the point of madness' and that we may not survive."

"But you know Baba and Sultan Burhan may send out search parties for us when they realize we are gone! Who is to say that they will not overtake us before we can escape to a place beyond their reach? Truly we would not survive the punishment we would suffer. And though you have set down your title for freedom, you are yet the queen. You care for our people, certainly more than Baba ever did. It would grieve you to the end of your days knowing that we could have stopped these vile criminals from terrorizing innocent subjects in our city, and instead did nothing."

Fatima scowled. Isla was right, but they were so close to freedom! Without asking, she was certain this plan would involve going back toward the city and tangling with the barbarians! She was also certain that if she refused, Isla would follow through with it alone. The fear of that was greater than her concern for her own safety, and so she grudgingly answered, "I have started on this perilous path. There is no point in me shying from risk and danger now. Tell me this plan."

Her worst fears were confirmed at her daughter's next words.

"Remember, I have gone further up the path than you, and had to return. I've seen what lies ahead, and it will aid us. But first we have to make our way back toward Chabouk."

Chapter Nine

Omar splashed cold water from the river on his face and scrubbed his eyes in the faint early morning light. As always, it took the eye with the scar a little longer to focus. Years after his fight with the palace guard who nearly took out that eye in some territory long forgotten, he still could not see clearly out of it. He could see enough to unseat an unwary traveler and divest him of his valuables and his life though. He rose and strode to the pallets to awaken his friend, so that they could be prepared for precisely such an adventure.

"Wake up, you sleepy-head before I haul you up by that ridiculous beard of yours! There's business to be about!"

He of the braided beard stretched stiffly and grumbled, "And a pleasant morning to you too."

The hulking bandit snickered in response as he started a fire. "You sleep late like an old woman while I have already caught our breakfast." He pulled out a sharp and sinister-looking knife and commenced to gutting a fresh trout. "Up with you and let us eat before we start our work."

Soon the fish was roasting over the flame. He reached into the flap of his satchel and pulled out a pack of spices he'd lifted from a shopkeeper.

Every so often he threw a bit on the trout and flipped it over. The smell grew more tantalizing and soon both their stomachs were growling in anticipation.

The moment it was done Omar made quick work of dividing it with his knife, and then he and Mustafa set to it enthusiastically, ignoring their burning fingers and tongues. A hunk of dry bread from last night's dinner split between them, a handful of chestnuts and fresh water from the stream made quite a satisfactory breakfast.

As soon as they put out their fire they were ready to fall upon whatever foolhardy traveler came their way.

As if on cue the most amazing thing happened! From the direction of Chabouk came two beautiful women strolling through the woods unescorted! Their arms were locked together and their heads leaned towards one another as they giggled and held some doubtlessly senseless council.

The men stared at each other in disbelief and then wicked grins snaked across their faces. These tasty morsels were fools or the city had grown lax to allow its citizens such liberties. Either way, they decided that this was going to be a most pleasant morning.

Their prey spotted them now and one woman gasped. She and her friend froze in their tracks with wide eyes and open mouths.

"A good day to you, my darlings," Mustafa crooned as he and Omar inched closer toward them. "What might such enchanting ladies as yourselves be doing unaccompanied in the forest?"

They could now recognize that the tallest was older than the other, but not less striking in her beauty.

The women appeared to realize the folly of their venture and the danger of their situation, for they glanced at each other and then hurriedly in the direction of the city.

"Run, Maman!" cried the younger one. Before they could flee, their attackers rushed forward. Omar grabbed the older one and Mustafa the younger. They meant to steal kisses and other... liberties but their victims fought like tigresses against their advances.

The bandits were surprised. These two yelled like warriors in battle rather than screaming like damsels in peril, as they fought for their lives. It seemed though, that they were too panicked to pay heed to their surroundings. Their struggle led them further from the safety of the city and closer to the river with its swift current.

"You've got spunk! I'll give you that," Mustafa chuckled as the young one twisted fiercely in his grasp. "I'll wager you have fire in your blood. It will be a pleasure to sample your wares." He drug her to his chest and crushed his lips to hers.

A moment later he howled in pain and let out a loud oath. She had bitten his lip and then spat on the ground. Blood dripped from the puncture, and before he could recover, she kneed him in the groin.

This time his cry was hoarse and full of agony. "You whore! I need none of your fire! Your flame needs cooling!"

With that he shoved her into the river. She shrieked in terror as she splashed about, battling to stay afloat as the current carried her away.

"Isla! My daughter!" the older woman cried out and fought against her enormous captor. "Oh please, pull her out! She will drown!"

"Surely she will," Omar replied, angry because they had not been able to have an early morning rut. "Now go and join her!" He pushed her into the channel and she too spluttered and flailed in vain against the river's flow as it rounded the bend.

Both women were nearly out of sight when they went under. They did not surface again.

Mustafa let loose an impressive string of foul oaths as he knelt to splash water on his offended lip. "Some adventures we've had this morning, and nothing to show for our troubles but bites and scratches."

"It would seem we have a little more than that," Omar said curiously. On the ground before him lay the embroidered sash the older woman had worn. It had come loose and fallen off in the struggle. It was adorned with tiny beads that formed a picture, and was clearly expensive. "This will fetch a nice price at the market, I'll wager."

"As will this," Mustafa exclaimed. As he'd prepared to stand at the river's edge he'd seen something sparkle. It was a bracelet that had been worn by the one called Isla. Gold, it was, and set with precious stones all around.

Omar eyed their treasures appreciatively. "This is truly a prosperous place for its citizens to stroll about in the woods wearing things such as these. Perhaps we might stay for a season and reap the plenty of the land, ay, my friend?"

Mustafa agreed. "I like the sound of that. We'll get more than we can imagine for these trinkets, and our day will end far differently than it began."

And so the plan was set in motion immediately. With no further thought to the women they'd sent to their doom mere moments before, they untied their horses and rode to Chabouk.

Chapter Ten

Sultan Shiraz was not having a very agreeable morning either. He and the royal family from Etmekstan had just arrived in the dining hall to break their fast. He was displeased to find his family absent and sent a servant to summon them immediately. After making a dismissive excuse about the folly of women he ordered the food to be brought in and served.

Dishes of pita bread, feta cheese, nuts, fruit and honey were placed on the table, along with tea and milk. Everyone piled their plates and commenced eating without waiting for the tardy women.

As the meal progressed the silence became increasingly uncomfortable as neither the ruler's family nor the messenger he had sent to fetch them appeared.

Panguian Cala murmured, "Tsk, tsk! Such disrespect for a wise and exalted leader such as yourself. Some women do not know their place," she chided as she gobbled up a piece of bread drizzled with honey.

"One of them shall learn hers very shortly," Mansoor grumbled under his breath, and then bit viciously into a juicy pomegranate and spat the seeds out on the floor.

His parents eyed him with censure but he sullenly ignored their displeased gazes.

The shame Fatima and Isla had brought on him caused Shiraz's puffy cheeks to grow hot and the color to rise in his face. Before he could speak, the servant ran into the hall, breathless after her futile search.

She knelt to whisper in her master's ear.

"What do you mean they are missing?" he bellowed, ruining all her efforts at discretion.

"A thousand pardons, Your Majesty. They are not in their rooms, which were bolted from within and had to be unlocked with the keys. The watchmen at the gate are certain they did not leave out by that route. They are not in the stables or the gardens or... or anywhere, Your Majesty. They are simply *gone*." She looked as if she would faint with fear, and bowed repeatedly.

Mansoor swore deeply and swiped his plate onto the floor. "Does she imagine that she can play me for the fool with coy, childish trickery such as this? I will not stand for it!"

"One would think," Cala said nastily, "that Princess Isla does not find my son sufficiently worthy of marriage."

Burhan rose so rapidly that he overturned his chair. "Now see here. If this is a jest, we do not find it amusing in the least. You assured me that this marriage would occur and we have traveled here in good faith. Now your family has gone missing? I will have a satisfactory answer for this puzzle."

Shiraz rose from his seat and yelled for the general to be summoned. Glaring at Burhan he spat "So will I!"

Within minutes, Commander Qasim arrived. Many a maidenly eye cast a longing glance at the handsome officer, dashing in his blue tunic, black trousers and boots. He took long, nimble strides to the table where his leader sat, and then in a single fluid move of his tall, graceful frame, he knelt on one knee and bowed. "I am at your service, Your Highness."

"The panguian and princess have apparently disappeared. I have been told that they cannot be located anywhere within these walls. I do not have to tell you what a serious situation this is or how speedily it must be remedied. Do whatever is required, but I expect them to be found within the hour!"

Qasim bowed his head and arose. "It shall be done, Your Majesty." He signaled for several sentries in the hall to follow him and he quickly issued his orders.

Soon thereafter, groups of two and three patrolmen mounted a search sweeping every cubit of the estate and fanning out into the city. Everywhere one looked their vibrant blue tunics could be seen. Though it was already midmorning, the glint from the sun reflected off the daggers that hung from their waists and made it appear as if nighttime stars sparkled in the marketplace.

The servers in the dining hall told the kitchen staff, and in minutes the mansion was abuzz. A fruit seller in the market overhead a set of patrolmen talking about the nature of their quest as they passed his stall. He ran and told the baker who told the tailor, and soon the news was all over the city.

By the time the breakfast dishes were cleared from the table and Shiraz had retreated to his bedchamber to sulk and fume, all of Chabouk knew that the queen and princess had vanished.

It did not go unnoticed by a couple of visitors to the market that everyone appeared to be in quite an uproar.

"I wonder what's going on here," said Mustafa, stroking his long, braided beard.

"I have no idea, but I don't like all these patrolmen marching about," Omar replied quietly, scanning the crowd.

Mustafa sighed. "Perhaps we should make our mina and be gone. I'd hoped to stay and rest here for a little while."

"We may yet be able to rest here. Whatever's going on might die down soon. Let us not give up hope yet."

They stopped at a vendor who sold men's footwear and offered to sell him a pair of pointed sandals they'd taken from the body of a past victim. As was customary, they haggled with him for a little while, mutually agreed upon a price, and he gave them shekels for shoes. In this manner they sold more of their purloined merchandise and eventually they arrived at a seller of ladies' garments.

They approached her and showed her the sash and bracelet.

She stared at the sash for several seconds. "What delightful material, and such fine quality. Surely you are distinguished merchants who have traveled from afar to bless us with such treasures. I will give you much gold for these items. Will that please you, sirs?"

"Indeed it will, old one," Omar chuckled.

"Excellent. These are worth more mina than I usually carry about with me, but do not worry. Jamilah! Come here, child," the woman called.

A girl of about ten summers, who had been playing in the street with her friends, ran over.

"Yes, grandmother?"

"Run home, fetch the extra bag of coins and bring it to me with haste."

The child's eyes darted to the two men and then she nodded. "Yes, grandmother!" and ran off in an instant.

"She will not be long. As we wait I will tell you of other merchants who will be happy to purchase your wares. You will have quite an eventful day, I'll wager." She motioned toward the street they had not yet traveled, and pointed out the types of stalls they would find and deals that could be had.

The bandits were so enthralled by the idea of the quantity of money they could pocket that they paid no attention to the flight of the girl.

She bolted through the streets until she found two officers who were searching for the king's wife and daughter.

"Please, come quickly! There are robbers at my grandmother's cart!"

One of the guards shook his head, though not unkindly, at the child. "We are on a greater quest than finding pickpockets this morning, young one. Our search is of royal importance." The soldiers started to move on but the girl's next words stopped them.

"Oh, please listen! My grandmother's request is too!" She breathed heavily from her running, and the urgency of her mission caused her to rush her words.

"She used t-to work in the palace years ago. She said that sometimes she recognized stolen goods from the sultan's house, and if ever she sent me home to fetch a bag of coins for a seller, that I m-must run with all my strength to find soldiers for there was a thief trying to sell things taken from the palace. Please come, for she just gave me those words!"

The guards glanced quickly at each other.

A petty thief was one thing but a robber who had stolen from the royal residence itself was another situation altogether. "Show us the way," one of them said, and strode briskly behind her as she set off running.

As they approached the cart they could make out a burly stranger and another with what appeared to be a rope swinging down the front of his ragged merchant's robe. The moment they realized that it was a beard they remembered their commander's warnings and descriptions of the roaming bandits. They quickly caught the attention of two of their comrades and signaled for them.

Because the old peddler was doing such a wonderful job gesturing and talking, the two false merchants did not notice the four armed guards approach until it was too late.

"Stand where you are if you value your lives!" the eldest soldier called, startling them.

"What seems to be the problem?" Mustafa asked calmly, although his heart beat wildly in his chest.

The woman answered calmly. "I am hoping you can explain to us whence you have come to own the royal sash of our beloved queen, who has gone missing as of late. She wears it only on special occasions. It is embroidered with the images of their Majesties on their wedding day."

The officer stepped forward and examined the cloth closely. "This is a serious charge. How can you be certain it belongs to the queen?"

"Because when I was younger I worked in the castle, waiting on her Majesty when she first arrived in Chabouk. It is since I have become too old to serve that I now sell the garments I sew here in the marketplace. I am quite crafty with my needle. It was I who sewed the sash and embroidered it with my own hands."

This was sufficient motive for the guards to take the men to the castle for questioning, and without even a chance to struggle, the outlaws found themselves being led by the ends of spears to the palace gates.

The commander was notified and delivered the message himself to his master. Within minutes, the monarch and his guests had assembled in the throne room and the two prisoners were brought in.

"Let me see the sash," Shiraz ordered. Qasim brought it forward and he inspected it. His face reddened and his eyes flew to the thieves. "This is indeed my wife's. Where did you get it?"

"Please, Your Highness," Mustafa bowed deeply. "We are simple merchants. We buy, sell and trade. We do not ask about the items' origins. Might someone have stolen it from Her Majesty's bedchamber and sold it?"

"No! Only a fool would sell something so easily identifiable." He stepped down from the dais and glowered at each of the robbers, neither of which could look him in the eye. His next words were so low as to almost be a growl. "And she was wearing it last night."

"Your Majesty, there is more in their packs, stolen no doubt," Qasim interjected. He dumped the contents of their satchels on the floor. Out fell all manner of clothing, small jewels, coins, knives and spices.

"They also tried to sell this gold bracelet to the peddler," the officer continued. "Might this belong to Princess Isla?"

At the mention of Isla's name, both men remembered that this was what the older woman had called the younger. They lost all color in their faces and could not help but stare at each other in disbelief. Of all the confounded luck, the women they had stumbled upon had been the sultan's own wife and daughter!

"Vile mongrels! Savage dogs!" Mansoor screamed as he jumped from his seat and snatched the bracelet out of the officer's grasp. "I gave the princess this bracelet as a betrothal gift upon our last visit to Chabouk!"

He would have attacked the prisoners but Burhan restrained him with great difficulty.

The prince fought to free himself from his father's grasp, and Burhan wondered belatedly if he had not shown enough discipline in the boy's upbringing.

"Be still!" he growled. "Let the king deal with these treacherous barbarians. The marriage has not yet taken place. If there is avenging to be done, it is yet his right."

Gasps of shock and dismay filled the court. If there was avenging to be done then the panguian and princess were... dead. Servants clasped each other's hands, and guards stood at attention with wide eyes and trembling legs.

The monarch shook with rage, but his voice was amazingly calm. "Your lives are already forfeit. You will meet your end before the sun has passed its peak this very day. Nothing you can do will spare you, but I may order a less torturous death if you tell me what you have done with my family."

The thieves looked at each other with eyes devoid of hope. Omar sighed. "We are undone. Your words ring true, old friend. We have found more than we expected here and this day will end differently than it began."

Mustafa swallowed and stared at the ground, unable to speak for the hollowness in his heart. They would die today.

Turning back to the sultan, the hulking man spoke the truth in a voice that sounded empty and lifeless to him. "We came upon them in the woods. They were walking and talking. We..." He could not seem to say 'tried to rape them' now that the husband and father of their victims stood before them. "They struggled with us. We... we threw them into a river that feeds into a great waterfall. They could not swim, and so they sank and did not surface again."

Panguian Cala gasped and covered her mouth. Workers cried quietly. This time two guards had to assist Sultan Burhan in holding his furious son back.

"Do you mean that those scratches on your faces," Shiraz wheezed, finding it difficult to catch a breath. "Are from my wife and daughter because *they were fighting to keep from being murdered?*"

Neither man could respond.

Commander Qasim hoped against hope, and begged to be allowed to ride with a unit of his soldiers to the waterfall in case the women had survived. They returned not an hour later, full of grief, and with a single drenched beaded slipper. It had been bobbing in the current near the base of the falls, where nobody could have survived the crushing weight of the rapids.

Though he thought nothing of disregarding his daughter's safety and happiness, or of beating his wife and planning her demise, the king found he could barely keep grasp of his sanity at the idea of their deaths by this common, worthless scum. The strength returned to his lungs and he shrieked. "I denounce my offer of lenient death! Your end will be slow, fearful and painful. I will have vengeance! To the stakes with them!"

The outlaws began to fight against their captors in earnest, for death by stake was a horrible thing. Omar cried out that his partner had thrown the princess in the river first, and begged for mercy. The betrayal made Mustafa furious and he shouted a grim litany of his partner's sins to counter his own. Their rants of treason against each other turned to pleas for mercy and cries of struggle that filled the air as their captors dragged them away.

The tragic news spread like ashes in the wind, and all across the kingdom citizens mourned for their kind and gentle mistresses.

Burhan offered the bereft Shiraz his family's condolences, praised him for ending the bandits' reign of terror, and assured him that they would all stand with him at the execution to see justice done.

That day, that very hour in fact, Omar and Mustafa's murderous raiding ended forever, as did their lives.

Chapter Eleven

"You know what is required of you. Now go, and do not fail me or you will regret it."

There was nearly a score of street urchins in the dank room at the orphanage. Some leaned against the peeling walls and others sat cross-legged on the cold, bare floor. Several of them cast their eyes downward and rubbed their backs. The welts there were a reminder of the manner in which the master punished failure.

One stripling in particular grimaced under the man's piercing glare. He was as unwashed and ragged as all the others, but he stood as tall and rail thin as his master. Had it occurred to him to try, he could have overtaken the man in a fight. But the cruel keeper of the orphans had instilled such fear in his charges from an early age that none dared cross him.

As the group shuffled outside, a dirty-faced youth named Ali jabbed the tall boy in the ribs. "Try to do something right for once, Tarh'ah. It was fun for a while to watch you get beaten all the time, but it's getting stale now."

The other children snickered and ran into the streets of Budmash.

Tarh'ah hung his head and followed, but more slowly. He had no liking for their task, and no amount of whipping could change his heart. By the time he got to the market the others had disappeared into the crowd, but he knew they were there, watching and waiting for an opportunity, as he was supposed to do. The master had trained them to be pickpockets. Their return to the orphanage with plenty of pilfered goods would earn them a second helping of dinner and a pallet to sleep on tonight. Those who failed to return with anything would get no dinner at all, a bed of scratchy hay and the end of the master's whip.

Poor Tarh'ah had gone to sleep hungry, uncomfortable and bruised countless nights, for he was a very poor thief. It pricked his conscious to steal from strangers who had done him no wrong. Most times when he had come back with anything it was because he had picked up coins on the ground to buy with; or a vendor had felt sorry for him and tossed him a piece of fruit; or he had sat on a corner out of sight of the other orphans and simply begged for alms.

At times he wished the kuipan would simply arrest and jail him. At least then he'd have a warm bed and a meal. Sadly it seemed to Tarh'ah that the man was blind to the young band of thieves' daily escapades.

(Although the kuipan was not blind he *was* corrupt. He conveniently turned a blind eye because he got a percentage of the profits after the keeper of the orphanage sold the goods his charges had stolen.)

Tarh'ah rounded a corner in time to spy three of the boys in an alley, taunting a fellow who looked to be about their age and size. His cream-colored turban, tunic and pants marked him as a trader's hireling. Ali, the one who had teased Tarh'ah, had figured his victim would have been trading and have a moneybag. He did not expect what happened when he tried to rob the boy. He was so fierce of spirit and fought so bravely that Ali alone could not subdue him, so the ruffian had called out for his friends and they had raced to his aid. This was the scene Tarh'ah happened upon.

A couple of them held the lad's arms so that he could not defend himself, and Ali punched him in the stomach. "What have you got to say for yourself now, dog?" Ali jeered as his prey doubled over in pain.

Tarh'ah's nostrils flared. It was bad enough that they were thieves who would slip a man's belongings from his tunic, but now they would also fall upon their innocent prey? He had to do something! He saw a moneybag on the ground and realized they'd taken it from the lad but set it down to have their fun with him. Tarh'ah snatched the bag up and jangled it around. It was heavy and the sound of coins was quite distinct. *Clink, clink, clink!* All the boys looked in his direction.

"I know who'll be having second helpings of dinner tonight," he teased.

A look of surprise flashed across Ali's face. "Give that here!" he yelled.

The distraction was all the poor servant needed. Using the boys who held him as a brace, he swung both legs forward, kicked Ali square in the chest, and sent him flying into the wall. With startling speed he twisted out of the grip of the others.

Tarh'ah tossed him the moneybag and then yelled "Run!"

Not needing to be told twice the youth bolted past the lanky boy who had saved him, slowing to look at him and say "Thank you!"

Tarh'ah darted in the opposite direction. There would be no second helpings tonight, or first helpings either. The thought of the awful punishment he would receive from the master made him swallow hard and tremble. No! He would not be ashamed! He had acted honorably!

If only he could escape this wretched place! He had dreamt of it countless times, just as he had dreamed of his family. He could not remember his maman but he had fleeting memories of his baba, a kind man who called him a name other than the one his master gave him. He had been quite small then, perhaps four or five summers when his father had fallen ill while traveling through Budmash. He never recovered, and the little child suddenly found himself an orphan in a strange place. All that kept him from going mad was the belief that once, someone had loved him. Perhaps if he could escape from here he might find a home again. But where would he go? Who would even care to help him, a sorry excuse for a thief in a band of fatherless waifs?

He made his way to the dung heap behind the stall where the animals were sold. The stench was nearly sickening, but at least none of the others would want to look for him there. To return to the orphanage now might very likely cost him his life. He would have to sleep in an alley, and avoid his master and the others for another week or so until tempers had calmed. So be it. He was used to being rejected.

That was, after all, what 'Tarh'ah' meant.

.

Chapter Twelve

"It appears that you have had a profitable day at market today," remarked the innkeeper to a lad who bounded up the stairs to his rented room with a stuffed moneybag. He could not have been more than twelve summers and he was full of cheek. He reminded the man of his own son and that caused him to smile whenever he saw the boy.

"Indeed! Won't you join me for a bit of innocent wagering so that it may be even more profitable, old man?"

The innkeeper guffawed good-naturedly. "I ought to box your ears, whelp! I've been gambling since long before you were toddling around showing your bare bottom. As if I would lose to a runt like you. Run to your baba before I decide to show you how it's done!"

The child smiled and disappeared around the corner at the top of the staircase.

After entering the room and locking the door, the youth abandoned the carefree façade the innkeeper had seen, and limped to the bedside of a resting figure. The turban came off and long, black hair tumbled to the waist of the 'boy.'

"Maman, I've returned. Are you well?"

Stirring from her slumber, the woman replied, "Oh, Isla! I'm so glad you have returned. I worry whenever you leave for the market."

Isla smiled weakly and slid to the floor against the wall, holding her stomach. That blow had knocked the wind out of her.

"What happened? Are you hurt?"

"I will be fine. Three street rats tried to rob me. Of course they assumed I was a boy so they fought me like one," she explained, leaving out the specifics. She rubbed her jaw gingerly and hoped it wouldn't swell. "You can bet that I gave them more than they bargained for, and an older boy helped me escape. They may go after him because of it. I hope he'll be safe."

Fatima's bruises and hard journey had taken quite a toll on her body. Nonetheless, she rose stiffly and went to kneel beside her daughter. "Let me see." She turned the girl's face from side to side, then pulled up her tunic and gently examined her. "There is not much bruising and I feel no broken bones. It will feel better after a couple of days."

Returning to the pallet she leaned against the wall. "Curse this wretched place! We cannot stay here any longer. There is no telling what other dangers await us here. There will not be sufficient light for us to reach Enamdar before night, so we must leave tomorrow."

Isla's heart raced and her face filled with worry. "But what Baba and those awful bandits did to you, all that traveling and climbing, and then the hard swim in the river – they've caused you to become so weak and ill. You need time to recover!"

Fatima arose stiffly and began packing their belongings.

"No. I can rest more when we arrive at Enamdar, where it is safer. We leave tomorrow."

Isla hung her head with guilt. "This is all my fault. Baba beat you because you dared to defend me. I wanted to ensure that nobody would follow us, and foil those bandits once and for all, so you went along with my plan. Then you were attacked again and had to swim with all your might so that we would follow the fork in the river that led to the road, not the waterfall. Now here you are, battered, bruised and feverish, and I am to blame!" She buried her face in her hands and succumbed to tears.

Fatima came and knelt by her once more. "No, my honey drop. I went to your father of my own will, because I love you. I am not sorry for that. As to your plan, it was exceedingly dangerous and abundantly foolish, and I lost a very nice slipper during our swim, but I believe it worked. We ensured that the sash and bracelet were loose and fell off in the struggle. I am sure they grabbed them as soon as they thought we'd drowned. It was my royal sash and your betrothal bracelet – everyone has seen us wear them. If those villains have tried to sell them at our bazaar, Commander Qasim no doubt already has them in his custody."

"Or worse, and it would serve them right. The bloodthirsty cutthroats," Isla murmured angrily as she crossed her arms.

Fatima chuckled. "Woe to the one who tries to cross you, my warrior. I do agree – I feel better believing that nobody else will die at their evil hands. Come now. Ask for our dinner to be sent up and then let us sleep. We will need our rest for the trip tomorrow."

They dined simply on small pieces of chicken, some half-cooked radishes, and bean soup without very many beans. It was a far cry from the sumptuous meals they'd had at home, but they rather preferred the taste of freedom than the finest seasoned lamb.

Isla stared at her plate in thought. "First Baba, and then Mansoor have proven again and again that they have no honor or mercy. I rather believe I don't ever want a husband. I find nothing noble or pleasing about marriage."

"Not all husbands, or fathers for that matter, are so heartless. There are those who care for their wives and children more than they do their own selves. It is said that Sultan Karim of Enamdar was loyal and loving until his wife died, and has always been an honorable father. Someday you will find a mate who will adore you and the children you bear him like that. Do not ever settle for less."

The girl's pain was too fresh to hope for such a thing just yet, so she changed the subject. "Why did Baba never take us to Enamdar?"

Fatima sighed. "Sultan Karim's domain is more prosperous than ours. That was reason enough for him to dislike it. He only kept company with rulers whose lands made ours look impressive by comparison, or who had something he wished to possess."

She chewed a piece of bread thoughtfully. "That was, of course, why he was so intent upon you marrying Mansoor. He knew he had not treated his subjects fairly. Enamdar's ruler has a reputation for being just and good. Shiraz always feared that Karim would rise up against him and overthrow him."

Isla set her bowl of soup down. "No matter how hard I try not to let it affect me, my heart still hurts when I remember that even though I was his own child, he viewed me only as a bargaining tool. In exchange for me, Sultan Burhan would have provided reinforcements in the event of a war that might never be waged."

"Ah, my honey drop, I understand that his disregard has scarred your heart, but know this: you are not a bargaining tool now. You are free. Embrace that and I believe your heart will heal after a while, as I believe mine will."

After their small meal they crawled into bed. Isla's soul ached and she blinked away tears. She knew the laborers' children used to envy her, but they couldn't have understood that she envied them too. They could play together while she sat alone. They could come and go as they pleased but she was a virtual prisoner within the confines of the mansion and its gardens. As they grew older they could court and flirt with whomever their heart fancied, yet she had been promised to an ogre who saw her as nothing more than an animal to be trained to do his will. In her mind their lives were richer than hers had ever been.

Her mother's love and the kindness of the servants had been her solace – that and being outdoors. She enjoyed climbing trees, swimming, practicing archery and anything else she wasn't supposed to do. It was her small way of rebelling against her confines and of finding her own sort of freedom.

She remembered her mother's words and was comforted. She was free now. She was no longer bound by rules of state dictating what she wore, where she went or what she could do. Her heartless father could not plan her life for his benefit without caring a jot for her feelings. She would never have to hide in fear from her brutish mate as her mother had been forced to do.

As her maman gently stroked her hair and hummed a soothing melody, the princess who was a princess no more murmured "We are free," and then drifted off to sleep.

Chapter Thirteen

An air of foreboding mingled with the spirit of mourning throughout the palace at Chabouk the following day. Something was not as it should be. The executions quelled the king's outrage less than many had presumed it would. He withdrew heavily into his cups for the remainder of the evening. By early morning he had summoned all the workers and soldiers into the courtyard. Even Magus, who had been ill as of late, had risen from his sickbed to be present. The royal family from Etmekstan was also in attendance, and was clearly uneasy about the mysterious proceedings.

Sultan Shiraz did not look well. Dark circles shadowed his eyes. He paced with an unhurried gait for several agonizing minutes, eyeing the large group with suspicion.

"I have pondered several things throughout the night, and I am still left with many questions. I am sure that with all of my *loyal* subjects within these walls," he said with mocking emphasis, "All mysteries will be solved this morning."

He moved to stand directly in front of Qasim. "How is it that my family – who has only been away from this kingdom on rare occasions, and then only on affairs of state with me – ended up wandering in the woods between here and accursed Budmash; yet none of my *vigilant* sentinels saw them leave?"

The commander winced. "I wish that I could give you an answer, Sire, but I do not know. I know only that each of my men takes his duties seriously, and would never knowingly allow the panguian and the princess to come to harm."

"Yet they *have* come to harm! The worst harm imaginable! You expect me to believe that none of your men were sleeping or drinking or whoring, but were all standing at attention throughout the night watch; yet my wife and daughter met their end outside the walls of my territory? Do you take me for a fool?"

Qasim straightened his spine and set his mouth in a grim line. "No, Your Majesty, but I believe in the honor of my men."

The ruler folded his arms across his chest and sneered. "I am glad you are so willing to defend these careless guards. Perhaps you are willing to defend them to the death? Hm?"

A shocked hush swept over the crowd. The officers glanced at each other uneasily. They took great pride in their service and in their leader. For many of them he was like a father. Would he be executed because nobody had seen the women slip from the castle?

The sentry who had escorted a battered Panguian Fatima to her chambers two nights past explained to his comrades in hushed tones of the brutal beating the king had given her. Many were aware that there had been several such beatings before. The officers started to wonder if their queen and princess had been attempting to flee, and with good reason.

"And what about you?" the ruler asked as he approached the group of chambermaids and singled out the one called Amani. "You were the panguian's personal attendant, yes? Do you mean to tell me that you were so busy tending to other things that you took no notice of your mistress' absence? What were you doing? Dallying with a groom? Stealing silver from the kitchen?"

"Please, my Lord," the maid cried as tears spilled down her cheeks. "I would not do such a thing! I have always served my lady faithfully and loved her, and the princess, dearly."

"Then if you were paying attention to your post, surely you must have an inkling of what happened." He circled her menacingly. "Women are foolish. They are always chattering. No doubt you noted my wife and daughter making some plan or other while you were serving so *faithfully*."

"No, Sire. They conversed about no such thing in my presence. I swear it!"

"I see," he replied, stroking his beard thoughtfully. "I wonder if you are prepared to swear on your life."

Amani had been the chief attendant for a long time now, since sweet old Yusrah had been too old to continue in that position, and had been fair and kind to the other workers. They covered their mouths in fear for her, worried, as the officers were, that their leader would soon meet her death.

Servants began to whisper about the fear the princess had of the cruel Prince Mansoor, and of their leader's callous disregard for her welfare. Many of them could understand why perhaps those noble ladies might have had to take flight.

Members of the crowd viewed their leader's erratic behavior suspiciously. The sound of murmuring grew.

He stalked to the front of the group, spun to glower at them and shrieked, "All of you are worthless! There will be a terrible price paid today for your negligence! I demand that the sentries who were on duty in the palace and at the gates when my family disappeared be arrested now! Arrest every chambermaid too! Do not think you can play me for a fool! Someone knows something! Perhaps a visit to the torture chamber will wring the truth out of you!"

"Your Highness, I beg you to reconsider," the vizier began as he hobbled toward his master.

But the king was in a rage. "Silence, you doddering old fool!" He lifted his burly fist and struck the advisor.

The man staggered and fell. Qasim stepped forward to help him up.

"Stand where you are!" Shiraz yelled as his wide-eyed gaze wandered to and fro over the crowd.

"Sire, the vizier is aged and fragile, and has served here since the reign of your father. I beg you, please allow me to assist him –"

"Enough!" the sultan roared. He pushed the officer back and grabbed his scimitar. Wielding it unsteadily he pointed the commander's own weapon towards him. "I have ordered arrests and they have not yet been carried out! You dare defy me?" His eyes were crazed now and he held the blade painfully close to the commander's neck.

"I see what is happening here! You are all conspiring against me!"

"I believe it is time for us to depart," Burhan said quietly to his family.

Cala pursed her lips in distaste and nodded in agreement. "The grief has obviously caused him to take leave of his senses. I do not like this strange assembly. Let us pack our things and be gone at once."

Mansoor spat on the ground, as he had a bad habit of doing. "Crazed fat fool," he muttered loudly enough for everyone to hear, and started to stalk away.

"You!" Shiraz barked at the prince. He turned from a greatly relieved Qasim and marched toward the youth. Those in the crowd scurried to move out of his path.

"A plague upon you and your blasted spitting, and throwing dishes, sulking about like a spoiled child, and disrespecting my home! I am Sultan of Chabouk and you are an insolent whelp who has not yet learned his place. You will learn it now!" With that the mad despot let loose a war cry and charged at the prince, waving the scimitar wildly.

Chapter Fourteen

The sun was just beginning to wash over the market at Budmash when Isla, in her costume, made her way through the streets. The vendors were preparing to start their day as she headed toward the livestock stall to buy a horse for the rest of their journey. The earlier they could leave the better.

Her mother apparently possessed a gift for assessing the worth of precious gems and metals. The handful of items she had picked for the girl to sell had fetched an impressive price, yet left more than enough valuables for them to sell for the final leg of their trip.

She had only gone a small distance when she heard a cough and a groan coming from an alley. Peering into the narrow passage she recognized the fellow who had helped her the day before! He was crumpled on the ground, badly beaten.

"Oh no!" she cried as she ran to his side. "I was afraid this might happen because of your bravery yesterday. Here, let me help you up."

She quickly assessed his injuries. His face had been pummeled rather badly and there were bruises on his limbs.

With some difficulty she got him to a standing position and, moving ever so gently, brought him to the inn. He could barely walk but he uttered not a single word of complaint. She was thankful that the market was still mostly empty as she half-walked, half-drug him through the street. She peeked into the dining hall and when she was sure the innkeeper was not there, she led him, step by agonizing step, up to the rented room.

By the time she got to the door Fatima had already opened it. "What is the commotion? What happened? Oh!" she exclaimed when she saw the condition of the stranger. "Here, bring him in!" She stepped aside to let Isla in, and together they both brought him to the bed and laid him in it.

Isla fetched a basin of water and brought it to the bedside, along with a cloth. "Here is my hero who saved me yesterday. I'm sure the others attacked him as revenge."

"I thank you for coming to my daughter's aid. We are in your debt."

The young man's eyes grew big as the "servant boy" slid off her turban. "You... you're a lady?" A look of admiration spread across his face. "You fight like a warrior!"

Isla didn't know what to make of that. She couldn't recall any males who had ever been impressed by her... undignified skills. She was at a complete loss for words and smiled as she rubbed her neck nervously.

Fatima stared at the girl as if she'd grown a third eye, and then turned her gaze to their charge.

"I believe you are the first person in the world to render her speechless."

He colored with embarrassment, unsure of whether or not he had done something wrong, but then Fatima giggled, and he was relieved to realize that he hadn't.

"Here, enough of this chatter. Let us fix you up," she said as she gently dabbed his face with the cool, soothing towel. She dipped the cloth again and again in the basin until all of his wounds and bruises were washed. Then she put salve that Isla had purchased for Fatima's own bruises onto his battered body.

He lay perfectly still, staring at her as if she were an angel. Isla wondered if anyone had ever shown him kindness. "What's your name?" she asked.

His eyes darted back to her and he cleared his throat. "Tarh'ah."

Fatima stopped rubbing salve on his arm and looked at him in shock. "Surely that cannot be what your parents named you."

He looked down. "I have no memories of my mother and I barely recall my baba. I know only that we were traveling through Budmash when I was very small, and he fell ill and died. I have lived at the orphanage ever since. It was the master that gave me the name because he says I am such a bad thief. It is not that I am bad at it," he said, lifting his chin defiantly. "It is that I refuse to do it."

"So that's it!" Isla exclaimed angrily. "The keeper of the orphanage makes the children steal for a living! I should have expected as much. This truly is a dreadful place!"

She approached the bedside and sat near him. "Because you helped me, you cannot go back, can you? They will kill you. They have already tried."

He swallowed and blinked back tears. "Yes. I stayed away all night, but they found me early this morning. I could have fought one or two, but there were five. They beat and kicked me and pelted me with stones for what I had done. They will do worse if I return, but I have nowhere else to go, and nobody to help me."

Isla shot a pleading glance at her mother, who hesitated only for a moment and then gave a subtle nod and a smile. Turning again to Tarh'ah she replied, "Yes, there is. We are leaving today for Enamdar, and from there on a voyage to a land far from here. You could depart with us."

He looked too afraid to hope. "B-but why would you do this?"

Isla smiled. "Because you saved me. We are on a hejira, fleeing for a better life. Our caravan is a bit small so we could use a larger number to make it a proper escape. Besides, you are in as much need of safe passage as we are. What do you say?"

His answer was to burst into tears until both women found themselves having to dab at their own eyes. When at last he could respond his only words were. "Thank you. Thank you."

Isla arose and began rewrapping her turban. "I'm going to get us breakfast before we leave. Before I do, we must do something about that awful name. You may have been rejected, but you are no more. What shall we call you?"

She tapped her chin with her finger for a moment. "I know. You weren't hard to bring here at all. We only had to move slowly because you were hurt. You probably don't weigh much more than I do. You were a light burden, so we shall call you that: Tehal. How do you feel about that?"

"Tehal," he repeated, turning the word over in his mouth. He gave her a lopsided grin that looked as if he hadn't used it before. "I like it very much." He looked out of the window and whispered his new name. "Tehal." Then he looked at his rescuers. "What are your names?"

The ladies glanced at each other, unsure of what to say. Had he heard of Chabouk's royal family? Would he recognize their names? He seemed trustworthy, but if he realized who they were, would he accidentally give them away?

He appeared to notice their discomfort and remembered that they were escaping some painful past as much as he was. "No worries. If we are all beginning afresh, perhaps we should all have new names."

The women's faces lit up.

"I like that idea," Fatima replied.

Isla nodded and smiled. "As do I. Well, Maman, this escape was your idea. You yearned for us to be masters of our own fate and now we are. What about that for a name?"

"Malika," Fatima answered, using the feminine word for 'master.' She smiled. "Yes, I rather like it. Now for you." Her face grew tender. "During my darkest days you were the bright star in my life and the song in my heart. Your name should be Lyra."

Isla clasped her hand and smiled. "Then Lyra it shall be."

With their new names the three put their old lives even further behind them, and thought of themselves as Fatima, Isla and Tarh'ah no more.

"Now, to celebrate our naming ceremony," Lyra continued, "I will see what food can be had to break our fast. Then when you are better, Tehal, we are off to Enamdar!"

Chapter Fifteen

It had taken Tehal another full day of rest and healing before he was able to travel. Only now he was sure he was going to be ill. The morning meal had been glorious, as were all the ones he'd had the day before. He could not remember eating so much at once. Now though, his stomach was turning as he and his companions rode through a ridge on the back of a camel. The saddle they were in rose and fell as the animal sauntered along the path, and that was what was making his stomach hurt so soon after his repast.

Lyra had originally intended to buy a horse to ride to Enamdar, but bringing him along had meant making alternate plans. Two horses would cost a great deal more, and besides, he had never ridden one and would have no idea how to climb onto it. It was Malika who suggested the camel as a means to carry all three of them, and to solve the problem of getting him atop their mount.

The huge beast had knelt and the group had climbed into the saddle. It was meant for two riders to sit comfortably, but the women were small and Tehal was reed thin and so they were able to manage fairly well. That was, at least until the camel rose up and launched into a trot. Since then, in the two hours since they'd departed, he had been terrified that he would fall off or lose his wonderful breakfast. Or both.

Even so, his heart was overflowing with joy. Budmash was behind him forever!

Lyra and her mother were dressed in their disguises and looked the part of a father and son if one didn't gaze too closely. They had also bought a set of clothes and a turban for him in the market. Lyra had jested that they should set up a stall in Enamdar and sell costumes. Malika had found that quite funny and he figured it pertained to their adventures before he met them.

Being freshly washed, well-fed and dressed in clean, fitting clothes had made him feel like someone else entirely. It was that young man that rode with his newfound friends straight through the streets and out of Budmash, with nobody even recognizing him!

He was Tarh'ah the rejected no more. Now he was Tehal the light burden. And he had a family of sorts. They had even said he could travel with them to a distant land! All that longing for escape and companionship – it was over now. At the thought he hastily swiped at the moisture building in his eyes.

Another thing that kept him from focusing on his rolling belly was the scenery. Budmash was a dusty brown flatland, but this was something he had not seen before. The ground was not level, but changed from lofty hills dotted with trees to low valleys covered in grass and flowers. He had not learned the names of all these things, but he knew they were more beautiful than anything he'd known existed.

Malika asked if he was faring well with the bumpy ride and he said he was fine even though he didn't feel that way. These ladies had been sent from heaven and he did not wish to do anything to displease them.

Apparently in addition to being a poor thief, he was also a poor liar. She chuckled at his reply. "You are 'fine' ay? I doubt that. My bones are aching horribly and my bottom is quite unhappy right now. Do not worry – you can tell the truth. You can always tell the truth to us."

That was different for him too: the freedom to say how he really felt rather than whatever would keep him from being rejected or beaten.

"Well, I *am* a bit dizzy from being so far up, and the rocking is churning the food I ate earlier. All the same, this place is wonderful and I am excited to get to Enamdar. I have heard several travelers speak of it, and I have longed to see it with my own eyes."

She assured him that it was an incredible sight to behold but warned him that he would have to endure the ride for quite a bit longer. Indeed they traveled for another hour before they stopped to eat their midday meal, which she had packed in a satchel before they left.

Tehal tried not to eat too much so his stomachache wouldn't return when they resumed their journey, but the cheese and bread and grapes were so tasty that he couldn't help himself. They washed it down with fresh, cool water from a stream and then climbed back atop the camel and continued on.

Nearly another hour had passed and Tehal had fallen asleep when Malika said "There! There is Enamdar!"

They had just climbed a crest and were descending into a valley when the place that was called "The Shining City by the Sea" came into view. None of them could talk, for the sight of it was wondrous!

The first thing they noticed was the sea itself. As far as the eye could see there was glistening water rolling in endless waves.

The majestic domed palace stood proudly at the peak of a crag. With its gleaming white walls and huge, colorful turrets, it was visible to sea merchants long before they arrived at port.

The group alighted at last and tethered their camel. After stretching and working the cramps out of their tired and bruised bodies, it was off to explore.

The houses in the village surrounding the palace were breathtaking at first sight as well. Pigment must have been plenteous there for the buildings were painted a variety of colors: Egyptian blue, yellow ochre, cinnabar, and the customary limestone.

The bazaar held every kind of wonder imaginable. There were rows of fragrant spices, fresh fruit and produce, and mouthwatering delicacies. Master jewelry makers sold their unique creations of precious metals and stones. Cart after cart teemed with exquisite Persian rugs, elaborately decorated pottery, colorful handspun clothing with embroidered designs, and shoes with intricate beadwork.

On one end of the marketplace was an impressive array of finely crafted weaponry, and stalls full of Arabian horses, camels, donkeys, sheep, goats and cattle. Upon reaching the other end visitors could listen to musicians perform in the streets, play games of chess or backgammon, or watch archery contests. Lyra watched in fascination as the archers skillfully hit their targets.

Malika smiled when she noticed the object of her daughter's attention. She declared that all their struggles and labors deserved a holiday, so the trio wandered around for the better part of the afternoon taking in all the sights, smells and sounds.

When they arrived at a stand that sold a dessert shaped exactly like an elephant's ear, Tehal's eyes grew so huge that Malika and Lyra laughed and said he must have one. They bought a couple and shared theirs but he was allowed to eat his all by himself. The fried dough was crunchy and covered with powdered sugar which he got all over his mouth. The ladies laughed at him even more then but he didn't care. He had never tasted anything so wonderful in his life.

Eventually they agreed to split up for a little while and meet again by the pastry stand. Lyra, of course, went to watch the archers again. Malika, as a former queen, had developed a keen eye for fine jewelry, and wandered to the booths containing gem-encrusted bracelets, silver belts and other such treasures.

As for Tehal, he could not get over viewing the sea for the first time, and when a massive merchant ship pulled slowly into port he was captivated all the more. He stumbled toward the shore as if in a trance, and watched intently as the crew unloaded its merchandise. He could make out spices and cloth, fruits and vegetables that were completely unfamiliar to him, casks of wine, and even livestock.

A crewman passing by with his load hoisted on his shoulder noticed Tehal's rapt attention. "You a sailor, young master?

"Me? No sir. I haven't been to sea before."

"Ah, that's it then. I had that same look in my eye when I was about your age and caught a glimpse of my first vessel. I'll wager you'll find yourself on board one of those before too long. I can tell that it's in your blood." The mariner chuckled good-naturedly and continued up the path toward the bazaar.

Tehal stared at the barge for a good while before he withdrew from the shore's edge and rejoined his companions. They wandered among the stalls until day turned to dusk. It was then that Malika sighed and spoke. "I am tired from all this traveling and we have spent many hours enjoying ourselves in the market today. We should find an inn, have dinner and get a good rest. Tomorrow we can sell enough to pay our fare and set sail for our grand adventure!"

Tehal gave that lopsided smile again. He had used it more times in this single day than he could remember ever having done before.

That night, after a delicious dinner he lay on a soft bed and sighed with contentment. So many nights in Budmash he had gone to bed lonely and hungry on a hard floor, wishing for someone to feel affection for him, even a little dry bread to eat, and a pallet to lie on.

But no more. Now he had a family, a full belly and a real bed.

He had no idea where Malika and Lyra had come from but they seemed as if their lives must have been unhappy before, as his own had been. He listened to them, on the other side of the curtain that divided the room, giggling with excitement as they discussed all the things they'd seen that day in the market. Then their talk turned to reverent whispers about their hopes and dreams for the adventures that would begin the following day when they cast off from the shore.

They eventually drifted into slumber, but he could not. He was too excited. The vision in his mind of sailing away on one of those magnificent boats on the morrow caused him to feel an emotion which he couldn't describe. It reminded him of the way the children had laughed and played in the streets that day. It was as if whatever feeling caused people to laugh was *inside* him. All he knew for sure was that it felt wonderful and he didn't want it to stop. When he fell asleep a while later, there was a lopsided smile on his face.

Chapter Sixteen

The next morning the three companions took their meal in their room where they could discuss the final part of their escape. They were so excited that they could barely eat.

"I heard so many languages that I could not understand in the market yesterday! I am beginning to realize that the world is bigger than I imagined!" Lyra exclaimed.

"Yes, I suppose I expected all people to use the same language. There is much about the world that I have to learn as well." said Tehal. "The sailor who spoke with me by the ship talks as we do though. I heard others on board talking about returning to Culgee today." He told them about the goods he observed being unloaded from the barge.

"I have heard of Culgee," Malika replied. "It is far to the west and can only be reached by sea. Imagine what an adventure that would be! To finally set eyes upon what is beyond the vast desert that cannot be crossed on foot or on the back of even the strongest camel!"

"It certainly appears to be prosperous by the variety of goods the merchants brought to sell," Lyra noted. "Perhaps we should hold onto what we have remaining rather than selling it at the bazaar today. Then we can see if they will allow us to depart with them as merchants. I say let us sail for Culgee!"

The others liked the idea and they prepared to leave immediately so they would not miss their chance to board the ship.

It was most unfortunate that when they got to the shore Tehal saw something gleaming in the sea and waded out to grab it. He couldn't swim but he wasn't afraid because the tide had only gotten to his ankles when he reached the object. It was a golden goblet simply floating in the sea! No sooner had he stepped back onto the sand than a pair of patrolmen approached him with their weapons pointed at him.

One of them stepped forward and extended his hand to a shocked Tehal. "Stop thief! Give that to me!"

He immediately surrendered the cup in wide-eyed fear, as his friends rushed to his side.

"Please, he is no thief! Do not arrest him!" Lyra pled.

The soldier eyed the merchant boy and the man who was presumably his master or his father. "Are you with him then? All of you will come with me."

The three travelers were miserable indeed as they trudged through the streets with soldiers on either side. Up the winding path they went, towards the enormous domed palace. Now that they could see the beautiful colored dwellings up close, that was far from their minds. What had they done? What would happen to them now? Would they be jailed? Each of them wondered these things with hearts full of fear. *Not now*, after all they'd gone through to get here! Not when they were so close to freedom!

As they were escorted through the main entryway they passed through a courtyard filled to overflowing with plants, flowers, trees and bubbling fountains. From there they entered the towering fortress doors which slammed shut ominously behind them. The onyx marble floor was cool beneath their feet. Huge windows let so much sunshine in throughout the hall that there was no need for the candles to be lit. Pots large enough for a person to hide inside sat in corners, massive paintings and rugs hung from the walls, and every so often they marched past an exotic-looking tiled sculpture.

People were scattered here and there throughout the hallways, and the high vaulted ceiling echoed with their quiet chatter. They glanced at the strangers with curiosity briefly and then continued with their conversations.

The group eventually stopped in front of another looming set of doors and waited with trembling knees as the guards conferred with the sentinel there. He nodded and slipped inside the door, closing it quietly behind him. Scant moments later he returned and motioned for them to enter the royal court.

Sultan Karim watched from his throne as the soldiers brought three men up the aisle. There were not many people at court today – only Raheem and Mahmood, Ihsan, his trusted vizier, his scribe and a handful of visitors of state; therefore, he saw no need to clear the chamber to handle whatever proceedings were necessary. He waited patiently until his men and their prisoners reached him and the lead soldier bowed.

"Your Majesty, in accordance with your decree regarding scavengers of the sunken vessel, we arrested these men. We caught him," he added, gesturing at the tallest of the three, "fishing this from the sea." He passed the goblet to the vizier and returned to his place beside the captives.

The king accepted the cup from his advisor, examined it, and then turned his gaze to the men. "You have heard the charges brought against you: scavenging for items rightfully belonging to survivors of the shipwreck in defiance of my decree. Do you have anything to say in defense of yourselves?"

The eldest one bowed. "Your Highness, we beg for mercy. We are no thieves." He stepped forward with his hands lifted in supplication.

The guard grabbed his arm and yanked him back. "Stay where you are. Not a step closer!" he barked.

The man cried out in pain and the one next to him turned and yelled "Release her! How dare you hurt her?"

Hushed chatter filled the room and Karim raised an eyebrow. "*Her*? Have I just heard you say 'her'?"

Amazingly, he who had spoken reached up and removed his turban, letting a cascade of ebony hair fall.

"By the stars! A woman!" a startled Prince Raheem exclaimed.

All eyes turned to the older man, who sighed and took off his turban too. Waist-length black and silver hair fell like silk.

The guard who had held the elder woman's arm in a vise-like grip immediately released her with a look of shock and embarrassment. "A thousand pardons!" he croaked.

There were more gasps from the crowd, and the sultan, who was suddenly having a most incredible morning, turned to the tallest one who had been accused of the theft. "What of you then? Are you a woman also?"

"No! I mean 'No, Your Highness!' " With a look of horror the fellow ripped off his turban to reveal a head of curly, short black hair. The indignation on his face caused a ripple of laughter in the crowd, and even the monarch had to fight back a smile.

Karim gazed with surprise at the women. "It appears I now have more questions to ask than I had imagined at the start. Let us begin with the most obvious: why are you ladies walking about disguised as men in my city?"

"Your Majesty," the older woman began. "We are travelers who have suffered many misfortunes. We felt it would be safer for us if nobody realized we were women."

He nodded. "Sadly in many places that is the case, but my domain is not such a place, I assure you. Women are respected here, so you may be at ease. Now why are you traveling without an escort in the first place? I can tell that this lad, while tall, is yet a youth. Have you no husband?"

The woman's gaze grew pained and distant before she replied "I will never lay eyes on my husband again, nor these children their father."

There was great sadness in the countenance of both youngsters, etched so deeply that the king felt in his heart it was real. "I am sorry for your loss. Can you explain why you have this?" he asked, holding up the goblet.

"Sire, there are more items in their bags," the guard interjected, and stepped forward with several pieces of jewelry, scarves and articles of women's clothing.

"Those are our own belongings," the older woman interjected. "Some of them are for our personal use and others were brought to be sold at the bazaar. Please, Your Highness." Her voice cracked and her eyes filled with tears. "These things are all we have left in this world besides each other."

"And they are not stolen," the tall one added. "I saw something shining in the water and went to see what it was. That's how I got it. Then these men arrived, called me a thief and arrested us." He stood with his back straight and his eyes firmly on the ruler. "I have been called a lot of things, and others have tried to force me to be many things, but I am not a thief."

The conviction Karim noted in the youth's eyes touched him. "No, I don't believe you are," he replied.

Ihsan stroked his beard, leaned forward and spoke softly into his leader's ear. "My Lord, might these be survivors of the shipwreck? Perhaps that is what happened to the husband, why they are unfamiliar with our city and have items of obviously great value. They might have been a family of merchants from the ship."

"Yes, Father," Prince Mahmood agreed in a quiet tone. "They are all bruised and move about like they are stiff or in pain. When the guard grabbed the older woman's arm she cried out, as if there were already an injury there. That would make sense if they had been battered about at sea."

Karim rubbed his chin. "That does make sense. What do you say, Raheem?"

"It seems likely to me, Father. They do appear to be of worthy character. Why not put it to them?"

The king nodded in agreement and turned from his private council to the three strangers. "I believe you are telling the truth. Tell me, are you from the vessel that sank off the coast three days past? A score of lives were lost. Was this husband and father you speak of among them, while you managed to survive that calamity?"

The girl answered passionately. "We have indeed survived misfortune and calamity, Your Eminence, and have had more adventure in the last three days than we would have ever imagined. We only wish to sail to Culgee to start our lives afresh and bring an end to the pain of our past."

"As I suspected," said the vizier. "We learned that the ill-fated barge was from Culgee, and its inhabitants indeed have our appearance and speak our language."

Karim watched the family intently. He knew in his heart that there was more to this story than was being told, and that the whole truth would be far more fascinating. Nevertheless, he was certain that they were good people with honest hearts, and that was enough for him.

"You are free to leave. I am sorry for the things you have had to endure. I give you my best wishes on your journey home." Turning to a soldier, he said "Have the treasurer provide them with sufficient gold for their voyage and extra to replenish their merchandise. The ship for Culgee leaves within the hour. Be sure they do not miss it."

The family bowed and the elder woman replied, "Thank you, Your Highness. May countless blessings be upon you and your household."

With that they were led away to make preparations for their trip.

As they were leaving out of the huge doors a sentry hurried in, fairly ran to the front of the chamber and bowed. "Sire, a messenger has traveled here at great speed with a dire request from Chabouk!"

Karim sighed. Sultan Shiraz was a harsh ruler whose subjects struggled more than they should have had to. A hurried rider from there seeking aid meant trouble. "Where is he?"

"He is waiting right outside, Your Highness. I will bring him at once."

Chapter Seventeen

The first thing Lyra saw as they stepped out of the royal court was the rich blue uniform of an officer from Chabouk. He was standing off to the side conversing with a soldier, and since they were flanked on either side by guards, he did not even notice them. Nonetheless she hastily ducked her head and glanced at her mother, whom she saw had done the same. Tehal was still too flustered from their ordeal to notice the worried look that had passed between his companions.

When they reached the area where they were to wait for the treasurer, the messenger had already entered the chamber they had stepped out of mere moments before.

"Wait here for a moment while I confer with the treasurer about your money," the soldier said as he stepped inside the treasury room and closed the door.

Tehal swallowed nervously, rubbed the back of his neck and stared at the floor. "I am sorry -"

"Be at ease," Malike interrupted. She clasped his hand, and when he looked up to meet her gaze she smiled. "Do you not see that you have done us greater service than harm?"

Lyra smiled at him too, and he released a sigh of relief. It would have torn him apart to have brought trouble upon them after all their kindness.

Agonizing minutes passed and still the guard did not return. Lyra was too nervous to speak. She stood with her arms crossed, tapping her foot impatiently. Why couldn't they leave now? What was taking so long?

Unable to bear the inactivity any longer, Malika paced the floor and Tehal wandered to a nearby window where he watched the sea.

A door opened and the women jumped from the noise after so much silence. Several of the people who had been in the royal court when they had arrived now emerged and dispersed into the outer hall.

Malika called out to a group who was scurrying by excitedly talking about whatever was going on. "What has happened?" she asked.

"What news!" one of the visitors exclaimed. She immediately scurried to where they were and appeared to be more than eager to share this fantastic piece of gossip. "You have perhaps heard of Chabouk?"

"Yes, I have heard it spoken of," Malika answered with a cool composure that Lyra felt was greatly to her credit.

"Well," the chatterbox began with a dramatic flourish. "An envoy from there just arrived to say that the king's family was killed by murderous bandits, and their deaths drove him mad! The outlaws were put to death but then he started commanding *everyone* to be executed – from the commander of his army to the lookouts that had been on watch to the chambermaids! Why, he even tried to kill the prince of Etmekstan with a scimitar! It required several soldiers to restrain him and keep him from starting a war with the ruler of Etmekstan! Thank the stars none of his people were killed. The vizier declared him insane and has had him confined to the farthest tower where he is now kept under constant guard!"

"Oh my!" Malika exclaimed with wide eyes. She leaned against the wall with her hand on her chest in genuine shock.

Lyra gasped loudly, and she knew her expression mirrored her mother's. Her plan had been successful, but even she could not have foreseen this turn of events!

Her mother finally recovered herself and stammered, "I... I am glad the bandits were caught and punished for their terrible crimes, and that nobody else was harmed, but why is the soldier here?"

The woman leaned in and whispered. "The people have no leader now, and a nation without a ruler is ripe for conquest. They are asking Sultan Karim to make their land his province, and it appears that he will grant their request! He is in counsel with his sons and the advisor at this very moment. Prince Raheem, as eldest and heir to the throne, must remain here, so his father may appoint his younger son, Mahmood, as governor there. I am certain that if he does this, one of the first orders of business will be to attend to accursed Budmash! That will be an immense relief to us all! Oh, this visit has been so exciting!"

With that she flitted away to further relay the spicy news.

A look of grim satisfaction settled over Malika's face. "So he who planned to falsely imprison me in a tower has become imprisoned there himself."

"And rightly so," Lyra answered. "And the conquest he most feared has come to pass by his own actions." She touched her mother's arm. "Are you alright?"

"Yes, I am," she replied after a moment. "Long have I wished for justice upon him. I am glad I was able to know of it, even if I could not witness it myself, before we leave." She glanced at Tehal, whose gaze had not wavered from the sea, and added softly, "Unless you wish to return instead of leaving. We could go back now, and take Tehal with us. You could rule as sultana. It has always been your birthright."

"I understand that you want me to have the things wrongfully denied me, but you have been denied much too – love and happiness and dignity. I know that in your heart, while you care for its people, you do not desire to go home again, now or ever."

Malika sighed. "No, in truth I do not. Every chamber, every hall, each piece of clothing or vase, would always remind me of the dark and empty life I spent there. Besides that, knowing that your father remained on the grounds would be most unsettling. It would only take a single guard who was on his side, and he could be aided in escaping. Then our lives could be forfeit, and we would not know it until it was too late."

They noticed that Tehal had snapped out of his reverie and was heading towards them. Quickly she added, "But I would go if it was your desire. I know that you would be a wise and compassionate ruler."

The boy reached them with his eyes aglow. "The sea! It is so beautiful! It's glorious! I never imagined..." he trailed off speaking, unable to find words to express his wonder, and turned his head again to the window.

At that moment the guard finally exited the treasury room and approached the three, who immediately turned to face him pensively. He handed Malika a heavy moneybag and gestured toward the entrance to the palace. "My men can escort you to the ship leaving for Culgee now."

"Many thanks," she replied. Then turning to her daughter she placed the moneybag in her hands, and gazed at her with adoration and complete confidence shining in her eyes. "The choice is yours, beloved."

Chapter Eighteen

"I am glad that Tehal has learned to keep his food down on such bumpy rides," Lyra said as she observed him standing wide-legged on the deck of the ship.

The captain of the vessel was the same man who had talked to him that day three weeks past in the bazaar at Enamdar. He had really taken to the lad and had been teaching him about sailing. Tehal had blossomed under the kindness and guidance of the sailor. That was not all that had blossomed. His lanky frame had begun to fill out since he'd been eating regularly, and all the hours he'd been spending on deck had deepened his swarthy complexion.

Malika chuckled as she watched Lyra steal subtle glances at him. "It is quite telling that since we've been on board this ship and could wear our own clothes again, he has barely been able to take his eyes off of you, as if you are an angel."

Lyra's cheeks grew warm. "Maman!"

"It is true! He is either learning from his new teacher, eating everything that is in sight, or gazing at you."

As if to prove her point, Tehal looked in their direction and gave Lyra a lopsided smile.

She returned the smile before he resumed his conversation with the captain, and then turned to find her mother smirking at her.

"Oh please, do stop!" She tried to be serious but ended up doing a poor job of hiding a smile.

"What? He is a good young man with a kind heart, and it looks to me that he will soon have a trade. He is no prince, but we have had enough of princes and sultans, have we not?" she added with a wink.

"Indeed we have!" Lyra agreed. "I wonder what happened to that beast, Mansoor."

"Oh, after word of what happened in Chabouk spreads throughout Bas I doubt any decent king will allow his daughter anywhere near him. Burhan and Cala will have great difficulty finding anyone who will have him."

The women giggled at that thought, but then Malika's smile faded.

"Are you sure this is what you want?"

Lyra laughed. "Yes, Maman, and you really must stop asking me that! My feelings are the same as when we left Enamdar. Baba had no intention that I should rule, so he refused to teach me. I would have had honorable intentions but no skill at being a proper sultana. Our people deserve better than that. Prince Mahmood has both experience and wisdom, and will be a wonderful governor. As Sultan Karim's province Chabouk will prosper as it never has. The poor will be poor no more and those wrongly imprisoned will be freed. All will be set right."

She grasped her mother's hands. "And now, we too are free. To live on our own terms, to be treated with respect, to live where we choose, in the manner we choose, and love whom we choose – that is what I want. You have already shown yourself to be skilled at appraising jewels. Think of the merchants that have already said they would do business with you when we land. And as for me," she added excitedly. "I heard there are female archers, hunters, animal breeders and horse trainers in Culgee! I have so many choices that I am having difficulty deciding what I will do. Imagine that!" she exclaimed as she hugged Malika, who chuckled at her exuberance.

"Very well, I believe you! I too am nearly bursting with joy and anticipation."

"We all are."

The women turned to find Tehal standing behind them. He had just walked up, and it was he who had spoken.

"The captain was right. You have sailing in your blood. You look happier than I have seen you since we began our hejira," Malika beamed.

"I do love the sea, but that is not the only reason. I hadn't even known what to call this feeling before, because I had not known the word 'happiness' in Budmash." He gazed fondly at them. "I am also happy because I have a family, because I am free, and because I have a whole new life spreading out before me." Turning to Lyra he added quietly. "The best day of my life was when you asked me to journey with you on your hejira."

She again found herself speechless at his words. She could only smile at him and then look away.

Malika made a sound that could have meant she was clearing her throat or snickering. Lyra couldn't tell which, and decided it was probably best to leave it alone. Her mother was enjoying this entirely too much.

A shout rang out, signaling that they were approaching land. The group fell silent as they watched the speck in the distance come more clearly into view. There were the reddish sands of the shore, green rolling hills and valleys covered with flowers and trees, and further away still were glorious towering mountains. Their home.

At last, Lyra found her tongue. "A new beginning," she declared reverently.

Malika's smile spread across her face as a rainbow does across the sky. "It is indeed."

Epilogue

Legends can begin in strange places. One such place was Chabouk, and it was the old seamstress who had foiled the murderous bandits who started it. When Prince Mahmood established himself in what had become the province of Enamdar, he learned of her brave deed and provided for her so that she did not have to work in the marketplace for the rest of her days.

Because of her fame she received numerous callers from throughout the village, and it was during those visits that she started to tell a tale. It began with a panguian and princess who fled a cruel sultan and an evil prince, but were drowned by the very robbers she herself had helped capture. The start of the tale was not the most interesting part though. It was the ending that captivated her visitors, for she always ended it in this manner:

"I think we should not grieve too much for them. After all, their bodies were never located, as is often the case when people are thrown into rivers and can swim."

How could she know this? In the same way that she knew the royal sash belonged to the sultan's wife: she had been her private maid for several years, and not just any maid. She was Yusrah, who had been there by the river on the day when her mistresses had learned to swim together.

The glory of this tale became as great as the story upon the tapestry in Isla's chamber which had inspired the great escape in the first place. The legend of the queen and the princess was whispered reverently among servants and children and those whose hearts were faint and needed courage in times of peril, in Chabouk and beyond.

Their story inspired hope and bravery for generations, which is as it should be, for that is how great legends are made.

About the Author

Deanna Stewart has been crafting tales of fantasy since childhood, where her lifelong love of mystical lands, magical powers and distant worlds began.

Hejira is her first novella, and the first story in her *Escape* series – a group of tales chronicling the exciting adventures of courageous people fighting to find freedom from oppression, and shape their own destinies.

Deanna lives in southeastern Wisconsin.

Learn more about Deanna and Enora Books at www.enorabooks.com.

Be on the lookout for two new releases
from Enora Books!

AB Johnson's anticipated first novel,
Breezes, is a tropical romantic mystery,
set on breathtaking St. Thomas,
U.S. Virgin Islands.

Flit the Fearless, the story of a daredevil
litte bird, is the premiere book of
children's author, Gabby Luckett.

Both books are coming soon!